BOOKS BY
ANTHONY POWELL

A Dance to the Music of Time, First Movement
(including the following three novels)
A Question of Upbringing   A Buyer's Market   The Acceptance World

A Dance to the Music of Time, Second Movement
(including the following three novels)
At Lady Molly's   Casanova's Chinese Restaurant   The Kindly Ones

A Dance to the Music of Time, Third Movement
(including the following three novels)
The Valley of Bones   The Soldier's Art   The Military Philosophers

A Dance to the Music of Time, Fourth Movement
(including the following three novels)
Books Do Furnish a Room   Temporary Kings   Hearing Secret Harmonies

OTHER NOVELS
Afternoon Men
Venusberg
From a View to a Death
Agents and Patients
Fisher King
O, How the Wheel Becomes It!
What's Become of Waring

OTHER WORKS
To Keep the Ball Rolling: The Memoirs of Anthony Powell
Volume I: Infants of the Spring
Volume II: Messengers of Day
Volume III: Faces in My Time
Volume IV: The Strangers Are All Gone
John Aubrey and His Friends
Brief Lives: And Other Selected Writings of John Aubrey
Miscellaneous Verdicts: Writing on Writers
Under Review: Further Writing on Writers, 1946–1990

PLAYS
The Garden God
The Rest I'll Whistle

WHAT'S BECOME OF WARING

A Novel

by
Anthony Powell

'What's become of Waring
Since he gave us all the slip,
Chose land-travel or seafaring,
Boots and chest or staff and scrip,
Rather than pace up and down
Any longer London-town?'

ROBERT BROWNING

THE UNIVERSITY OF CHICAGO PRESS

For
EDITH

The University of Chicago Press, Chicago 60637
Copyright © 1939 by Anthony Powell
All rights reserved
Originally published in 1939
University of Chicago Press edition 2014
Printed in the United States of America

23 22 21 20 19 18 17 16 15 14   1 2 3 4 5

ISBN-13: 978-0-226-13718-6 (paper)
ISBN-13: 978-0-226-13721-6 (e-book)
DOI: 10.7208/chicago/9780226137216.001.0001

Library of Congress Cataloging-in-Publication Data

Powell, Anthony, 1905–2000, author.
    What's become of Waring / by Anthony Powell.
    pages cm
    ISBN 978-0-226-13718-6 (pbk. : alk. paper) — ISBN 978-0-226-13721-6
(e-book)
    I. Title.
    PR6031.074W47 2014
    823'.912—dc23

                                                                2013033837

♾ This paper meets the requirements of ANSI/NISO Z39.48-1992
(Permanence of Paper).

1

I WAS sitting in the Guards' Chapel under the terra-cotta lunette which contains the Centurion saying to one, Go, and he goeth; and to another, Come, and he cometh; and to his servant, Do this, and he doeth it. The occasion was the wedding of a girl called Fitzgibbon who was marrying a young man in the Coldstream. The incident took place during the address. As the parson was approaching the end of his discourse something flicked through the air and landed in my hat resting brim upwards on the pew beside me. On examination the object turned out to be a page torn from the service paper, folded several times and inscribed in pencil: *Put all your money under the seat or I'll drill a hole through you.* It was signed *Red-handed Mike* above a skull-and-crossbones.

The exceptional circumstances of the arrival and contents of this missive at such a juncture in such a place was some preparation, when, after choosing a suitable moment, I glanced over my shoulder, for the sight of Eustace Bromwich sitting two rows back. At the same time his presence was unexpected because he was said to be travelling in the Near East. Dark red in the face, with gleaming white eyeballs, he was staring severely at the altar as if presiding over a court-martial which had to try a particularly disagreeable case. He made no sign of recognition except for frowning and brushing up slightly the left-hand half of his moustache. The dowagers on either side of him, and beyond them the field-marshal with his nieces, sat impassive, so that Eustace's communication had escaped their notice.

The rest of the service passed without interruption. The register was signed while the choir sang Handel's *Where'ere you walk*. From the confusion of sage-green and dull gold the wedding march from *Lohengrin,* executed by a cluster of crimson musicians, growled out through the pillars. There was a wait while the photographers did their business; and the crowd began to struggle towards the doors of that extravagant Lombardian interior, which always seems like a place you are shown round after the revolution, the guide pointing out celebrities among the carved names, rather than a church in regular use. The congregation hung about for a while among the sad, tattered colours and glittering Victorian blazonry, until they were disgorged at last from under the massive pediment on to the barrack square.

Eustace was on the steps outside. He was wearing a grey top-hat and looked more dapper than ever. Dapper and a shade melancholy, standing there with the sun beating down on the asphalt and the elephant-coloured barracks behind him like the background to a satirical print of which he was the subject. His enormous histrionic gifts were quite apparent even in repose.

'My God, I never thought they'd let me in there again,' he said. 'Not for a moment.'

'They must have regretted doing so in view of your behaviour.'

'Are you going to the reception?'

'Only for a few moments. I have to get back to the office.'

'Still advertising?'

'I'm a publisher now.'

'Who with?'

2

'Judkins & Judkins.'

'Whom do you prefer? Judkins? Or Judkins?'

'Judkins, emphatically.'

'How is the life of that French fellow going?'

'It progresses slowly.'

'I have a bus somewhere here,' said Eustace. 'You had better come with me.'

We walked across towards the cars parked in rows under the control of policemen and non-commissioned officers. One of the N.C.O.s opened the door of a Rolls as we approached it.

'Get in,' said Eustace, and, turning to the soldier, he said: 'You used to be right-hand man in my company.'

'Sir?'

'Isn't your name Madgwick?'

'Sir.'

'Do you remember me?'

'It's Captain Bromwich, isn't it, sir?'

'It is,' said Eustace. 'Congratulations on your stripes. Go and drink my health in a quart.'

The man took the half-crown and saluted. Eustace got into the car. He drove at the gates as if he meant to smash through or jump them. We turned left, making for Cadogan Square.

'I shan't forget that fellow in a hurry,' Eustace said; 'he stank like Abraham. Seeing him makes me glad I left the Army.'

'You must be very prosperous, Eustace, to own a car like this.'

'Just off the starvation line. This car is lent me by an American woman. She even wanted to marry me. In my present financial position I can't afford to be too particular, but I had to draw the line there.'

'What are you doing now?'

'Collecting the remnants of the once vast Bromwich fortune, with which I propose to buy a boat and end my days sailing about the Mediterranean.'

'I didn't know you attended weddings any more.'

'Between ourselves, old boy, I'm not sure that it wasn't my daughter's. After all, one has one's duties as a parent, I suppose. Anyway, I happened to run into the girl's mother in Bond Street the other morning. She talked about the Old Days and said how young I was looking and asked me if I would come. You know I can never refuse a woman, so there it was. But I expect it is the last time I shall ever wear these clothes.'

No one could ever tell when Eustace was giving an imitation and when a confidence. He threw himself with such heart and soul into his impersonations of splenetic generals, White Russians, Cockney privates, and Levantine panders that for the moment he actually became them; so that it was not possible to judge whether he was revealing a scandal of twenty years before; or whether his voice had become suddenly that of some brother officer, famous in the regiment for boasts of this sort.

'You're not often in London now.'

'I have an old great-aunt who is going to leave me a few hundreds. When things look bad she sends for me. She says she can't live for ever. I think she's wrong.'

'Where have you been all this time? You were last heard of creating a disturbance in the bazaar at Aleppo.'

'I visited China since then. And Tibet.'

'We're publishing a new book about Tibet.'

'Who by?'

'T. T. Waring, whom you've no doubt heard of.'

'Of course I've heard of him,' said Eustace. 'That fellow gets into my hair. What do you think of his writing? I suppose he makes a lot of money out of his books.'

4

'He does pretty well. So do we. He seems to get around to a lot of places people haven't visited before.'

'If he ever crosses my path,' said Eustace, 'I shall tell the little beast what I think of him. Half the hardships he brags about are what the ordinary tourist puts up with as soon as he has left the Blue Train, and sometimes before.'

'The public don't think so.'

'Then they must be a lot of damned fools. Talking of books, have you seen anything of Roberta lately? She is supposed to be writing one.'

'Not for ages. I don't know what she can be doing.'

'I always have a warm corner for Roberta,' Eustace said; 'and I think she used to be rather fond of me too. I must try and get hold of her before I go abroad.'

Eustace and I had met first a year or two before at the flat of a girl called Roberta Payne, when his Army career was already at an end. Eustace had joined the regiment about eighteen months before the outbreak of war. He had served at one time and another on most of the fronts; and in Siberia and Asia Minor after the Armistice. It had been a career not without stormy passages. Since his retirement Eustace spent his time travelling, when he was not riding, sailing, gambling, or reading. He often complained that money was getting too short for him to indulge freely in any but the last of these hobbies. This was not surprising, as he spent it copiously. As we drove along he said:

'I haven't decided yet where I shall make my head-quarters. When I do, you will have to come out and see me there.'

'I might look you up one summer.'

'Don't delay too long or I shall have made the place too hot to hold me.'

'It will be a French port, I suppose.'

'Yes, I'm going to make myself the scourge of the Côte d'Azur.'

When we arrived at the house where the reception was taking place he disappeared in the crowd. I wanted to write down his address, but Hugh Judkins had some things to discuss that afternoon, and it was already late, so that after a glass of champagne I had to slip away from the drawing-room without having a further opportunity to talk to Eustace about his plans.

Downstairs the hall of the house in Cadogan Square was full of men and women. More were streaming up the steps. It was astonishing that any two people could have so many friends and relations. A girl a short way ahead was also trying to make her way out into the street. As we reached the door together I recognised her as Roberta Payne.

'I'm on my way to Fleet Street,' she said. 'Let's share a taxi.'

'I'm not going to Fleet Street. I'm for Bloomsbury.'

'Come some of the way. I'll drop you.'

We found a taxi.

'Did you see Eustace? He was enquiring after you.'

'I spoke to him for a second,' Roberta said, 'but a mass of people shoved their way between us. I didn't see him again. He said he was going to live in France. I've just come back from there.'

'What part?'

'The south. I can't tell you how lovely it was. It was awful having to go back to the old paper.'

Roberta was a tall girl with large black eyes which had a trick of increasing in area when she looked at you. Her way of walking was also provocative. She always made a lot of fuss about her poverty and her journalism. The little articles she wrote were often amusing, but they could not possibly have kept her alive. She was usually so well housed and dressed that it was generally supposed that obscure rich men, too dull to be allowed to appear, contributed something to her upkeep. At least, she was believed never to have love-affairs within her own circle of friends. That was what people said about her. Roberta was a charming creature, though you could rarely believe all she told you.

'You know, I'm thinking of writing my memoirs,' she said, as we moved east in the taxi. 'I shall be twenty-five next year and I've had an adventurous life. Do you think Judkins & Judkins would like to publish them?'

'I'm sure they would.'

'Of course there are some things I could only hint at. But I think that is all the public expect these days. They like a good deal left to the imagination. It is so much more exciting than what actually happens.'

'Where would you begin?'

'With my parents,' Roberta said. 'A lot of people think that my father murdered my mother. I don't believe that for a moment. But he used to what's called "pass on" horses when we lived in the country, and I must say some pretty funny things sometimes happened. And then there was all the business of why he left the Yeomanry.'

'It sounds fascinating.'

'It was,' said Roberta. 'And even the story of how we lost all our money is by no means without interest.'

She sighed. No one could ever agree as to the relative truth of Roberta's stories about having been brought up in an Elizabethan manor house in Yorkshire.

'Have you got anything good coming out soon?' she said. 'I haven't read anything amusing for ages.'

'Odds and ends. An attack on theosophy. A book of Welsh proverbs with lino-cuts.'

'A new T. T. Waring?'

'Yes, there's going to be a new T. T. Waring. About Tibet.'

'I shall look forward to seeing it,' Roberta said. 'Will you let me know when it is due?'

'I'll send you a prospectus.'

Soon after this I handed over some money to Roberta, said good-bye, and took a bus up Kingsway. Roberta kept the taxi to pay a round of visits on editors, of whom she knew an unusually large number.

The post of reader to the firm of Judkins & Judkins was poorly paid, but not uninteresting. I had been with them for about a year. It was a small business with two partners, Hugh and Bernard Judkins, who were brothers. The house, founded by their father, Eli Judkins, for publishing text-books and works of a serious nature, had drifted gradually into general publishing, because neither Bernard nor Paul (a third brother now dead) had the energy to keep up this specialised line. Hugh had only come into the firm after Paul's death. Before that he had been an assistant master at a small public school. Old Eli had been a Nonconformist business man and his two elder sons had spent their lives consolidating their social position, but Hugh, who was about ten years younger than Bernard, had always had revolutionary ideas. Until Paul died he had refused to join the firm. When he did so in order to keep the business in the hands of the Judkins family, he threw himself heart and soul into a profession which provided boundless scope for the intellectual fussing that he had found so congenial as a schoolmaster. He saw to it that Judkins & Judkins became a flourishing concern again.

From the day that Hugh entered the office, Bernard, never over-addicted to optimism, became increasingly embittered. He dated from the period when a reasonable standard of

8

honesty and good manners were the best that any writer could hope for from his publisher—and even these were hard enough to obtain. As the years went by, such assets, adequately provided by himself and his brother Paul, had become of less and less value in competition with large advances and newspaper advertising. Bernard began to loathe books, so that it seemed he had only entered the trade to take his revenge on them. His life (he was about fifty-five when Paul died) became one long crusade against the printed word. Every work that appeared under the Judkins & Judkins colophon did so in the teeth of Bernard's bitter opposition. Hugh, who had always disapproved of his elder brother's worldly ambitions, did not take this sort of thing lying down. If Bernard could annoy him by refusing to publish authors Hugh wanted, there were ways in which Hugh could annoy Bernard. He did not hesitate to employ such methods.

At the period when Hugh offered me the job at Judkins & Judkins I was a copy-writer at an advertising agent's and wanted more time to work at a book I was writing on Stendhal. It was a surprise when Hugh made the suggestion, because we had met only two or three times. He had said that he himself was an admirer of Stendhal. This must have influenced him in making the decision. Bernard showed no enthusiasm, but made no active objection to my joining the staff.

There was still something distinctly pedagogic about the way Hugh Judkins spoke to anyone under the age of twenty-five. Perhaps it was because of this that he was particularly good with young authors. He made under-graduates and others, newly arrived in London, feel that they were important. Not that he disliked the opposite sex. On the contrary, women of any age made him blush and talk excitedly as if he had suddenly fallen in love. He

9

was unmarried and I had never heard a breath of scandal about his private life. Hugh had a thin moss of sandy hair where his head was not bald, and flashing rimless pince-nez which he wore lashed to one ear by a chain.

The offices of Judkins & Judkins were in one of the Bloomsbury squares. The rooms were spacious, with good mouldings and first-rate door-knobs of the period. Hugh's room was the smaller half of what had been designed originally as the drawing-room. It was divided from Bernard's sphere of influence by folding-doors which were kept for ever bolted. The effect of this was that if anyone spoke louder than a conversational murmur they could be overheard on the farther side of the partition. Hugh used to complain about this often; but it gave him an opportunity for seeing that Bernard arranged nothing behind his back. On the whole he preferred the risk of Bernard getting wind of his own plans to foregoing the advantage of hearing what his brother spoke in an angry or excited moment. Bernard spent most of the day dozing or conning the weekly papers, so that the gain was almost always to Hugh, who had too constant a stream of visitors for Bernard to keep track of them even if he had felt inclined to do so.

That afternoon Hugh had a number of things he wanted to discuss. I sat in his room for over an hour going through manuscripts with him. When we came to the end he pushed back his chair and opened the window. Staring out at the square, he said:

'Did I hear you telling Peppercorn last night that you had never seen a medium in action?'

'You probably did.'

The previous night I had dined with Hugh and an assorted collection of authors and agents. The conversation had turned on spiritualism, and Hugh had changed the subject quickly. In some respects a sceptical character, he had one interest about which he was a trifle coy, not to say secretive. He liked going to séances. I had been told this by other people. Hugh himself had never before spoken of such matters.

'Of course I don't exactly believe in spirits or anything like that,' he said, 'but these alleged phenomena have an interesting side. I attend an occasional sitting. I wondered if you would like to come with me one night, since you have never been present at anything of the sort.'

'Very much indeed.'

'I'll see if I can arrange it,' said Hugh. 'It won't be in the immediate future, because for various reasons nothing much is going on at the present moment—largely because our chief organiser has gone into a nursing-home. But later on.'

'I shall look forward to it.'

'They are nothing much, you know. I'm afraid you will be disappointed,' said Hugh, laughing awkwardly, as if he had said something indecent that he regretted having allowed himself to mention; and changing the subject he went on: 'By the way, the new T. T. Waring has been delayed. It is annoying, but there it is. Let's hope it will be a big success when it does arrive.'

'Let's hope so.'

'How is your Stendhal getting along?'

'Slowly.'

'Has it got a title yet?'

'*Stendhal: and Some Thoughts on Violence.*'

'Ah?'

It was always a surprise to be reminded that Hugh was a Stendhalian. Later I began to understand better what he found to satisfy him in the Frenchman's writings. They shared, of course, an admiration for Italy. Not that Hugh

ever showed any signs of regarding Italians as Noble
Savages. He once said that it was the frankness about the
author's frequent failures in love that appealed to him. I
suspected a sympathy with Stendhal's belief that power was
the foremost of pleasures. It can hardly have been an
interest in seduction considered as a science.

2

SOME months passed. I thought that Hugh had forgotten about his invitation or decided that he had been indiscreet. However, in the early spring of the following year he asked me to accompany him on one of his jaunts into the occult. It was arranged that we should meet at his flat for a glass of sherry and a sandwich before the function.

Hugh's flat was on the ground floor of a red-brick pile near Baker Street. To reach the door one clattered along a black-and-white stone passage, feeling like the last pawn left at a game of chess. It might have been thought that no one of his own free will could live in this building who had not drunk of despair to the dregs; but Hugh and the other people I knew who inhabited these mansions (another publisher and his wife, and Peppercorn, the literary agent) were never tired of praising their beauty and convenience. Here Hugh did a good deal of entertaining, in which even the most misanthropic publishers are forced to indulge if they want to make a success of their business. Hugh was far from being a misanthrope. He managed to get a lot of fun out of his gift, which amounted almost to genius, of inviting to dinner guests of an antipathetic temperament.

When I arrived he was waiting in the sitting-room, with the decanter already poised above a glass. He was dressed in a thick pepper-and-salt suit with a butterfly collar and knitted tie. Everything seemed a trifle too big for his rather miniature frame. The general effect suggested academic prosperity. I was a couple of minutes late. Hugh gave his accustomed grin, half uneasy, half reproving, as if this unpunctuality had already spoilt the evening for him, but he was prepared to bear no malice. We had not met all that day because there had been a Board meeting at the office. Hugh's face gave warning that all had not gone well at this conference. Almost at once he said:

'I'm having a difficult time with Bernard. He is being very obstinate.'

'What is it this time?'

'I want a laid paper for Mrs. Gulliver-Lawson. He insists on a wove.'

'How very annoying.'

'And besides there were other things too. Silly old fellow.'

It sounded as if the Board meeting had been a bitter one. Since Hugh had joined the family business he had been inclined to treat Bernard's office as a sort of ante-chamber to Bernard's tomb. Bernard resented this. Paul, the middle brother, when he died had been nearer Hugh's age than Bernard's. Bernard was fond of drawing attention to this.

'Anything good among the manuscripts?' Hugh said, altering his tone of voice with heavy insistence and pretending to be cheerful.

Evidently he had been thoroughly annoyed by Bernard but did not want to do more than mention what had happened.

'Nothing.'

'I wish the new T. T. Waring would come along. It is due any day now. We want something to buck things up.'

He munched a sandwich with neurotic violence. The champing of his teeth gave the impression that they had eluded their owner's control and that nothing short of a

14

crowbar would put a stop to their crunching attrition.

'You must look at that American novel we asked for,' Hugh said. 'I want your opinion on some of the passages that will have to come out. I'll give it to you tomorrow.'

'*Campus Stooge*'?

'No, I've decided we can't do that. *Lot's Hometown*. It came in yesterday. But we mustn't talk shop. Let me tell you something about what we are going to see.'

I should have liked to hear more about the row with Bernard. In such matters I acted as Hugh's hired assassin, as it was he who had got me the job. In business it is important to know how matters are going, as employers are of capricious temper and may decide without warning that they need a creature with qualifications of a different sort from one's own. However, the story would no doubt be revealed in due course. Hugh said:

'We are going to the house of an American widow who is interested in—in these matters——' Hugh could never bring himself to call it 'spiritualism', and he had almost as much difficulty in speaking of 'psychical research' because it sounded too dignified. His feeling of guilt about the whole concern, derived no doubt from his Puritan heredity, forced him to belittle the importance of his diversion. '—a man named Lipfield organises them. He is my stockbroker, as a matter of fact. You may find some of it rather dull, but the medium seems a fairly reliable fellow, so that if the curtain does twitch it isn't necessarily attached to his foot.'

Hugh paused and laughed to show that the affair was not to be taken too seriously. He said:

'It usually turns out to be a draught under the door if anything like that does happen.'

'I see.'

'We'd better be starting now,' Hugh said, sniffing to remove some crumbs from immediately beneath his nose. 'Lipfield always likes everyone to be punctual.'

'What is our hostess's name?'

'Mrs. Cromwell.'

We set out along the echoing corridor and picked up a taxi from the rank near the entrance to the flats. Hugh told the driver an address in Kensington. On the way we talked of business, a subject never far from Hugh's mind. A couple of first novels had been failures. Hugh said that he wanted to be cautious about fiction in the near future. He also sketched out a scheme for a series of modern travellers to be sold at four shillings. In making plans of this sort his energy was tremendous. He said:

'Of course it would be with an eye to T. T. Waring in the long run. The new one has got to be a real winner. I want to see his sales double.'

The taxi stopped in front of a large stucco house. There was a bit of garden in front of it with a sundial and some lead gnomes. Hugh went up the steps and rang the bell. A parlourmaid in a lavender uniform and mob-cap opened the door. We were taken through the hall to a back room on the ground floor where eight or nine men and women were standing about in groups talking. The furniture and decoration of the house were expensive, not in bad taste but with the gloomy air of having been bought wholesale from a reliable antique-dealer. Lipfield, Hugh's stock-broker, a fat, energetic man, introduced me hastily to our hostess and the rest of the party.

Mrs. Cromwell was a more impressive figure than might have been expected. She was tall and thin and had certainly been good-looking in her youth, if not a beauty. Her hair was a regular silver-grey with a curiously wig-like appearance. It was set above a sallow, almost almond-coloured face made up to conceal a web of small wrinkles like the veins in a leaf. She looked about sixty and was very gracious.

There were a few minutes of conversation. Then we all followed Lipfield into a further room, the walls, ceiling, and floor of which had been covered with the same mauve material. A semicircle of chairs faced a black curtain. The medium, a slim young man with an inquisitive nose and weak double chin, sat in a dressing-gown opposite the last chair at the far end from that at which I found myself. My neighbours were a man introduced as Captain Hudson, who wore a blue suit and a moustache but otherwise left no visual impression; and a withered lady called Miss M'Kechnie, of whom Hugh sometimes spoke. She was an old acquaintance he had known in his schoolmastering days, the aunt of one of his pupils with whom he continued to keep up. They were said to quarrel whenever they came across each other; but never badly enough for relations to be severed finally. Beyond Miss M'Kechnie sat an ex-official who had administered some African territory —someone said he had been a district-commissioner in the Sudan; and next to him was Hugh.

The lights were extinguished except for one that played on the curtain's fold and enclosed in a glowing circle a tambourine, a mandolin, and a trumpet. We held hands and waited for a little attention on the part of the dead.

The medium went under control with a good deal of puffing and blowing. After a few minutes he spoke a few phrases in a small high voice like a child's. This happened several times with long silences in between. The spirit sought was that of George Eliot. On previous occasions she had announced that she wished to be called Mimi, so it was by the latter name that she was addressed by Lipfield in his periodical appeals to her to take some notice of Mrs. Cromwell and her guests.

Tonight Mimi seemed unwilling to commit herself on any subject in spite of wheedling remarks from Lipfield, who acted throughout the proceedings as master of the ceremonies, and sporadic bursts of singing from the assembled party. Once or twice the curtain flickered, but, as Hugh had said before we arrived, this appeared to be the result of draught rather than the work of Mimi or her familiars.

Towards the end of the second hour I began to feel hungry. There had been an interval for coffee, during which I had a long talk with Lipfield, who took a lot of trouble to explain all that had gone before at previous sittings, but the effect of this stimulant was wearing off. From time to time Captain Hudson's hand contracted in a slight squeeze. He was evidently suffering from nerves. On the other side Miss M'Kechnie's mummified paw seemed to have become part of me. It was as if she were there for life: an elderly Siamese twin. At the far end of the row of chairs a woman began to cough. I heard Hugh clearing his throat. Then Lipfield's voice, sounding as if it came rolling out of a loud-speaker, said:

'Perhaps we might try another song. Mimi seems a shade sulky tonight.'

Miss M'Kechnie leant forward towards the spotlight. Her brittle nails ran into my palm.

'Dear Mimi,' she said, 'shall we sing for you, Mimi?'

'Come on,' said Lipfield, '*Little Brown Jug.*'

'What about *Loch Lomond* for a change?' said the man from the Sudan. 'We haven't had that for some time.'

'No,' said Lipfield, 'I think Mimi likes *Little Brown Jug* best.'

The man from the Sudan persisted.

'We had some good results from *Loch Lomond* the last time we sang it,' he said.

'We will sing *Little Brown Jug* now,' said Lipfield. 'Perhaps we might sing *Loch Lomond* later—if there is time. Come on, everybody.'

He led the singing:

'If I'd a cow that gave such milk
I'd clothe her in the finest silk;
I'd feed her on the choicest hay;
And milk her forty times a day.
Ha, ha, ha, you and me,
Little Brown Jug, don't I love thee;
Ha, ha, ha, you and me,
Little Brown Jug, don't I love thee.'

There was a pause. The woman near the end of the row began to cough again. Captain Hudson's hand gave several faint twitches.

'*Dear* Mimi,' said Miss M'Kechnie. Her voice quavered a little.

'Sssh,' said Lipfield. 'Something's happening.'

A noise of panting came from where the medium sat, facing the last chair of the line. Then a faint squeaky sound like rubbing a wet cork on the surface of a bottle. After that there was silence for several minutes. The Sudanese district-commissioner began to breathe stertorously.

'*Tee-tee,*' said Miss M'Kechnie. 'Mimi said *tee-tee* again.'

'I can't understand her at all tonight,' Lipfield said. 'However, isn't it about time to close down?'

Everybody except Miss M'Kechnie seemed agreed to call it a day. There was another wait while the medium came from under control, snorting for a time like a steam-engine.

'Will somebody turn the light on?' Lipfield said, when the last sobbing, agonised gasp had subsided.

19

Ungrappling myself from Miss M'Kechnie, who clung on as if she hoped that tenacity might be rewarded by some further manifestation from The Other Side, I blinked round the mauve room. In one corner half a dozen framed automatic drawings leant in a pile against a blackboard. There were no windows. The people stood up one by one. Talking to each other in low voices as if they were in church, they passed into the ante-room where we had drunk our coffee. The medium reknotted the cord of his dressing-gown, while with his head a little on one side he listened to something that Lipfield was telling him.

'Gasper?' said Captain Hudson, offering me his case.

'Come in and have some refreshment,' said Lipfield, sweeping us through the door. 'After you, sir.'

The coffee-cups had been cleared away in the ante-room and lemonade and biscuits were set out on the table. We stood about while these were handed round. Apart from the persons already mentioned there were two or there well-dressed women, middle-aged to elderly, and a man with grey hair and a copper-coloured face who looked as if he might be a retired naval officer. Lipfield seemed to have them all under his thumb.

'Do you often come to these—these shows?'

Captain Hudson said this. He was about thirty or perhaps a year or two more, rather below the average in height, with broad shoulders and pale blue eyes. His appearance suggested Scotch blood. He looked deadly serious.

'This is the first time.'

'Interested?'

'In a general way.'

'Lipfield suggested I should come,' Captain Hudson said, 'as I'd never been before either.'

He seemed to feel that he owed the world some explanation for being in such a place, and that by telling me why he was there he was making a sort of public amends for a social irregularity.

'How did you like it?'

'Rather like a visit to the cinema,' he said. He was not giving anything away.

In a convex mirror that hung above the mantelpiece Hugh's reflection appeared. He was crossing the room. When he reached the fireplace he took off his pince-nez and began to polish the glasses, half closing his eyes as he did so. Then he bared his teeth, making them click gently, and put on his pince-nez again, coiling the guy rope round his ear. He stared hard at Hudson.

'Well?' he said. 'How did you like it?'

'Parts of it were excellent, I thought. Captain Hudson here tells me that it was his first experience too.'

Hugh eyed Hudson again. He said:

'I had an idea he was new to it. I must warn him not to be taken in by all people say about these sittings. I sometimes attend them, but of course I am completely sceptical.'

After saying this he stared round the room challengingly. No one took any notice of the remark except Lipfield, who had come to the mantelpiece to look for matches.

'My dear fellow, we all approach the subject in a spirit of scientific enquiry, I hope,' Lipfield said. 'That is what we are here for.—Isn't it, Mr. Pemberthy?'

The man from the Sudan rubbed his hands together.

'Some pretty odd things happen,' he said. 'One can't deny that.'

Hugh bridled. For a moment his body seemed to vibrate from head to foot. He said:

'You won't think that when you have seen a bit more of it.'

'Mr. Pemberthy has been going to sittings for twenty years,' said Lipfield.

He assumed a judicial expression as he said this which implied an effort to prevent Hugh from making more of a fool of himself than he had done already.

'Most of them when I was on leave, of course, though we did arrange one in Khartoum on Twelfth Night once,' said Pemberthy. 'I can tell you I have seen and heard some pretty odd things.'

Hugh shook his head. He said:

'All mumbo-jumbo, the whole bag of tricks. I haven't been doing it for twenty years, but I've done it long enough to discover that.'

'Still,' said Lipfield, finding the match-box at last, 'you continue to come.'

'Oh, yes,' Hugh said, laughing in his most provoking way. 'I like mocking at you all.'

Lipfield was about to answer when everyone's attention was directed to Miss M'Kechnie, who put down her glass of lemonade and gave a little scream. To command silence she held up in the air a bridge-roll.

'I *know* what Mimi wanted to tell,' she said. 'I've guessed what it was. Mimi was saying T. T.'

'We all heard that,' Lipfield said. 'It is of no use to us if we don't understand what it means.'

'But I *do* know,' said Miss M'Kechnie. 'Mimi means T. T. Waring, of course.'

'What? The writer?'

Hugh gave an irritable start. Miss M'Kechnie said:

'Something has happened to him. Mimi was trying to warn us.'

For the moment this interpretation of Mimi's message put an end to conversation. The silence lasted for several seconds. Then Pemberthy said:

'Ashamed of my bad education and all that, but who is T. T. Waring? Never heard of him to the best of my knowledge and belief.'

'Such is fame,' said Hugh, removing with a bandana handkerchief some traces of lemonade from the lapel of his coat, together with a crumb or two that remained from the earlier snack.

Several people began to tell Pemberthy about T. T. Waring, making it clear that African exile did not excuse ignorance of such an order. They were cut short by Hugh, who said:

'Perhaps as I am T. T. Waring's publisher I should explain who he is, since it seems to be necessary. And also what he stands for.'

'I've already gathered that he is a sort of explorer and that he was chosen for the book of the something and that he is young and very modest,' said Pemberthy, who seemed not so much nettled by everyone's efforts to put him right as overwhelmed by the sheer volume of words that assailed him. He added: 'T. T. Waring sounds a sporty boy to me if the story about the priest's loin-cloth is true. But I don't see what he has to do with Mimi.'

'T. T. Waring,' said Hugh, embarking on one of his favourite subjects, 'is a challenge. I think he is symptomatic of something that is taking place in England today. You see, he belongs to the generation after the post-post-war generation.'

Hugh stopped and cleared his throat. He looked round the room as if he felt he had gone too far and expected to be contradicted. Mrs. Cromwell helped him out.

'Oh, but he's such a Puck,' she said. 'He gets me with his colourful stories. I just can't resist that T. T. Waring manner. There's something so virile about him too. And then all that philosophy.'

23

'Anyway, I don't see what Mimi wants to drag him in for,' said Pemberthy. 'Don't forget that Mimi is George Eliot. We only call her Mimi because she asked us to.'

Miss M'Kechnie said:

'I do not think you need worry yourself, Mr. Pemberthy. Mimi will make her meaning clear in her own good time.'

As everyone would have to wait until the next meeting to find out whether or not Mimi could be relied upon to explain herself there was a silence. This was broken by Captain Hudson saying with diffidence:

'There was something on the posters about the death of an author. Perhaps it will turn out to be T. T. Waring. I hope not.'

'Nonsense,' said Hugh with startling violence. He had a habit of swallowing in the middle of his sentences when he was excited, and he went on in a series of gulps: 'T. T. Waring is as fit as a fiddle. I heard from him only a month or two ago. Besides, he has a manuscript for delivery. It will arrive any day now. A book that should be a big success.'

'Oh, I don't expect this was T. T. Waring for a moment,' Captain Hudson said. He seemed surprised at the effect of his remark.

'No, no,' said Hugh, 'of course not.'

Miss M'Kechnie pressed together her lips in a way that gave them an obnoxious grinning expression. She said:

'I shall wait to hear what Mimi has to say at our next sitting.'

'You may have to wait a long time,' said Hugh.

He laughed a lot after saying this to show that he was joking. Miss M'Kechnie said nothing; but she nodded her head sourly several times.

'Well, I'll let you all know about Wednesday week,' said Lipfield.

He was standing in the doorway and seemed anxious to get home. Some of the other guests complained of fatigue. The party began to break-up. Hugh and I said good-bye to Mrs. Cromwell and went to look for our coats and hats.

Making a literary reputation—as Hugh was fond of saying—had never been so easy as in the dozen years after the War; nor keeping one—he was accustomed to add—so difficult. For this reason people have forgotten about T. T. Waring because most of his readers were of the kind who find authors' names hard to remember; while the critics who praised him so highly cannot devote space to an old favourite with so many fresh works of genius waiting for their due. His collected works were 'remaindered' almost as soon as they appeared. Ships' libraries and the Caledonian Market are the last resting-places of the original copies which have not fallen out of their bindings. All the same, T. T. Waring sold well when the going was good. He was compared with everyone who had ever written a successful travel book, Burton, Doughty, Hudson, and the rest of them, the accents of all of whom were certainly to be caught in his own works. He was the brightest jewel in Judkins & Judkins' crowd, a diadem that Hugh, with some reason, had recently begun to regard as his own personal piece of regalia.

T. T. Waring came to Judkins & Judkins through Peppercorn, the literary agent. Peppercorn, who had been described as one of Nature's literary agents, owned a small business which he conducted himself. One day he had called on Hugh with a travel book that had been issued by a firm of hedge-publishers, a shady concern living on books of verse paid for by their authors, bolstered up by an occasional illustrated treatise on sexual psychology. This

25

firm was in liquidation, and the book, T. T. Waring's first, having gone to a second edition, was one of their few assets. Peppercorn had his reasons for offering it to Judkins & Judkins rather than to one of the bigger publishing houses. T. T. Waring had signed a contract that made it by no means certain who now owned the rights of his work. Taking it over meant spending money, risking legal proceedings, and putting a lot of work into something that might show little or no return.

This was one of the occasions when Hugh showed his business ability. He took a fancy to the book at once— it was about wanderings in the interior of Ceylon—and he went to considerable trouble to straighten matters out in order that T. T. Waring should become a Judkins & Judkins author. He was successful. The following year T. T. Waring's second book appeared. It went into three impressions. About two years before I came into the firm the T. T. Waring legend began to form.

T. T. Waring himself never appeared. It was even suggested that Waring was not his real name. His manuscripts were sent to Peppercorn, usually from abroad, together with detailed instructions as to how they were to be produced and suggestions for advance publicity. These suggestions were little masterpieces of self-advertisement. Certain critics were not to be sent review copies because they were 'frivolous'; various persons in the public eye for one reason or another—preachers, actors, business men, and an assorted collection of politicians of all parties —were to be presented with the book at the author's expense on account of his 'admiration' for them; portraits showing T. T. in different outfits were produced, with instructions that they were to be supplied only to papers that dealt regularly with topics of geographical interest and on no account to those occupied for the most part with

26

'society gossip'; orders were given that his 'modesty' was to be plugged all along the line. In short, by the time his third book appeared, T. T. Waring had shown himself to be a master of the science of building up a literary personality. His sales increased by leaps and bounds.

The public liked T. T. Waring because (to quote Hugh again when speaking of another author) he was the almost perfect exemplar of a form of woolly writing that appeals irresistibly to uncritical palates; but how Hugh and others, who had had every advantage of education and prided themselves on their taste in letters, could stomach those tinny echoes of a biblical style, much diluted with popular journalism, it was hard to guess. Perhaps in Hugh's case it was because he invested with romance any book taken on by himself which made a financial success. However, he had some substantial critics on his side, and as there is no way of proving that writing is good or bad, and as T. T. Waring admirers shouted much louder than his detractors, he must be allowed to have had skill of a sort. In spite of some who echoed what Eustace had said about him, there were many who thought that T. T. Waring must be a remarkable traveller even though they did not like his writing.

As T. T. Waring went from strength to strength Hugh's delight in him increased proportionately. When the early books had appeared Hugh had admitted that he found some of the digressions dull, and even silly, and that it was not easy to sort out episodes in chronological order. But now that there were six or seven Warings in the catalogue and they covered Asia, Africa, America, and the South Seas, Hugh placed them above criticism. T. T. Waring was exalted in his mind to the incarnation of Youth Triumphant, the sort of figure photographed on the cover of magazines advising Germany for your Holiday. It was a form of adolescent hero-worship that Hugh must have caught from his pupils when he was a pedagogue; but even Bernard, who had naturally felt opposed to the whole business from the start, was forced to admit that T. T. Waring's sales had caused a distinct improvement in the monthly turn-over.

Other publishers tried to lure T. T. Waring away with offers of a bigger advance or a higher rate of royalty. He always reported their intrigues to Hugh, with whom he corresponded regularly. Although he used such occasions to get a bit more money, he seemed happy to remain with the firm. More than once in his letters he expressed a preference for a small concern where a lot of trouble was taken with his work rather than one of the large companies where he would be only one of several best-sellers. It was therefore not to be wondered at that Hugh was disturbed by the suggestion that some ill had befallen his special pet of the Judkins & Judkins list.

Captain Hudson had stopped to light his pipe outside Mrs. Cromwell's house. As Hugh and I came down the steps we nearly ran into him. The pipe began to draw at this moment and all three of us walked together along the street. For a time no one spoke.

'Where exactly are we?'

'I'm pretty well lost,' Hudson said. 'I came with Lipfield in a taxi. He goes home in the other direction.'

'I think the Boltons are through there,' Hugh said. 'Cheerful neighbourhood, isn't it?'

He laughed, making a noise like water hissing from a siphon. He said to Hudson:

'My family used to live in this part of the world when we were children. I have a flat near Baker Street now.

It's more convenient. Does Lipfield manage your stocks and shares?'

'No.'

'You're a soldier, aren't you? At least I presume you are too young to be a naval captain. Besides, your moustache.'

Hugh gave his laugh again. Hudson said:

'I am adjutant to the Territorials Lipfield is in.'

'Indeed?'

'That was why he asked me along.'

'What is your regiment?'

'Westmoreland Fusiliers.'

Hudson spoke gruffly. He must have thought Hugh inquisitive.

'Yes, yes,' Hugh said. 'I remember now Lipfield telling me that he was a Territorial. I was an officer in the O.T.C. myself for a short time. I had to give it up for health reasons. I thought that was a lot of nonsense about T. T. Waring this evening, didn't you?'

'Bit unconvincing.'

'You know all about him, of course?'

'As a matter of fact I am one of his great admirers,' Hudson said. 'I have every book he has ever written.'

Hugh was pleased. I could tell from the way he talked to Hudson that he liked him. It was a lucky chance that Hudson should turn out to be something so dear to Hugh as a T. T. Waring fan. He said:

'Which is your favourite?'

'I liked the first one as well as any,' Hudson said; 'and after that the one about Arabia. But I like them all. When is there a new Waring coming along?'

'Soon,' said Hugh, 'any time now. I expect it will be very good. You know, it is my great ambition to persuade him to visit England one day. If he does you must come

29

and meet him. The trouble is that he is so lacking in proper pride that he is afraid of being fêted.'

'There is a theory that you ought never to meet your favourite author,' I said.

'I'd take a risk on that with T. T. Waring,' Hudson said. 'By Jove, I'd give something to meet that fellow.'

'We must see what can be done,' said Hugh. 'I think that bus takes me to the place where I am going to play a little bridge before I go to bed, so I'll say good-night.'

'Good-night.'

'Good-night, Hugh, and thank you for the party.'

We watched him hurry off. The bus began to move just before he reached it. The hidden agency that seemed to have towed him towards it gave Hugh a sharp tug that brought him on board, yanked him up the stairs and removed him from sight, all in one rapid movement.

Hudson and I ploughed our way on through South Kensington. The night was warm and the stagnant character of those streets seemed to communicate itself to one's limbs and hamper progress. It was like crossing a marsh Suddenly Hudson said:

'Why not come to my place and have a drink? I've got some beer, I think.'

'I'd like to.'

'Let's see how we can approach it without taking a taxi,' he said. 'I'm saving up to get married.'

Hudson lived at the top of a block of offices in Victoria Street. We climbed several flights of stairs and turned off down a dark passage at the end of which a sink had been built into an alcove that stood beside a door. Hudson opened the door. He led the way into a room somehow Moorish in effect. The far end was curtained off. The curtain had not been fully drawn, so that part of a brass bedstead could be seen beyond it, and a wash-stand against which rested a bag of golf-clubs and a sword in a leather scabbard-case. Coloured pictures of famous hunts hung round the end used as a sitting-room. Hudson said:

'It isn't any great shakes up here. I've only got it furnished for the duration of my job.'

I sat down on one of the battered arm-chairs. Hudson went to look for the beer, which was kept, so it appeared, in the bathroom. There were a pile of books on the table, most of them in old bindings, a map, and some sheets of foolscap covered with pencil notes. A framed snapshot of a girl stood on the cupboard. I examined it and thought the face seemed familiar. Hudson came back into the room. He saw me looking at the photograph.

'That's Beryl,' he said. 'What do you think of her?'

'She's not called Beryl Pimley, is she?'

'You know her, then?'

'I used to know the Pimleys. I haven't seen them for years.'

'How damned funny!'

'They used to give tennis-parties when they lived on Salisbury Plain. I was still at school. Beryl was the pretty one.'

Hudson's whole manner had changed. Up to now he had been distantly friendly, always keeping a slight rasp in his voice. He seemed delighted to find someone who had met the girl he was going to marry, for this was who she must be. When I knew him better he admitted that he felt lonely in London. His family lived in the north of England and most of his friends seemed to be in his own regiment, one battalion of which was in India and the other at Catterick, so that he did not get much chance of seeing them. When he came back from the Territorial headquarters he rarely went out except to take part in the social life of the unit itself. He had no acquaintances apart from those with whom his work brought him in contact. Although he would never have owned up to it, he must sometimes have felt heartily sick of Lipfield and his other Territorial officers. He said:

'The father was a sapper, you know. They made him a major-general after he left Southern Command. He is retired now. They have a house near Camberley. Yes, as you say, Beryl is the pretty one. Poor old Winefred doesn't seem to make much going.'

He poured out some beer and sat down.

'That really is damned funny, you knowing the Pimleys,' he said. 'Beryl and I are going to get married this summer before I go back to the regiment. That will be in about eighteen months' time. We've been engaged for nearly two years.'

I did not remember much about the Pimleys, whom I had not seen for about ten years. They had two daughters. The elder, Beryl, Hudson's girl, must be now about thirty. She had been considered 'pretty' in the circles in which they lived; while her sister Winefred was thought to be unusually 'plain'. In these circles such judgments were regulated by traditional concepts of physical beauty. In a less conservative society than that provided by local tennis-parties Beryl would not have graded so high for her looks; nor Winefred so low. All the same, Beryl was above the average in this respect, while Winefred, unless she was improved, had a discouraging exterior. She was about two years younger than Beryl. I could recall lank hair and an alarming way of leaning forward and showing her teeth at anyone she engaged in conversation. Their father was a small worn man who looked as if he were perpetually worried about money. There was little to differentiate the

Pimleys from hundreds of other families of the same sort. Hudson appeared suited in every respect to marry one of their daughters.

'Who was the chap we came away with this evening?' Hudson said. 'Do you know him well?'

'Hugh Judkins. He is one of the partners in the publishing firm I work in.'

'So you are in it too. Have *you* ever met T. T. Waring?'

'No one has ever met him. That is his great strength.'

'What a wonderful time someone like that must have,' Hudson said, 'while we potter about here, trying to earn a living. My God, I can't help envying chaps like that sometimes.'

That was the earliest indication that Hudson gave of the profound romanticism that regulated his life. He spoke bitterly.

'I suppose you could get transferred somewhere if you liked. You'll probably go to India anyway, won't you?'

'Oh well——' Hudson made a movement with his hand. 'It isn't the same, you know. After all, the Army is the Army everywhere. Besides, one would be married, I suppose, and all that. Anyway——"

Neither of us spoke for a minute or two. It was not clear whether he was really expressing a thwarted desire for a life of adventure or giving vent to day-dreams of a glamorous East of painted cardboard and tinkling temple bells. He changed the subject suddenly by saying:

'Still, I suppose one shouldn't grumble. You know, I'm a bit of a writer myself in a small way.'

He laughed and pointed to the books and papers on the table.

'A novel?'

'Oh, come off it. I couldn't write a novel. No, it's a sort of history of the regiment, as a matter of fact. An unofficial one. I'm doing it more for my own amusement than for any other reason.'

He showed me some of the books he was working from. In one of these were several pages of typescript describing fighting in the Burmese wars.

'May I read this?'

'I shouldn't bother if I were you.'

All the same, he seemed flattered that someone should want to read something that he had written.

'It is pieced together from a diary I came across,' he said.

I began to read the typescript. Clichés are harder to avoid in military history than in any other form of narrative writing. To describe a battle in a readable manner needs a marked talent. There seemed no reason to expect more than the usual mechanical phrases in Hudson's account of the Westmorelands' engagement. But this prognosis was wrong. The style was lively and clear. Hudson was a dark horse.

'That is to be fitted in later, of course,' he said. 'I came across it by chance. At present I am only at the beginning of the eighteenth century, when we were Colonel Knatch-bull's Foot.'

'It will take a long time to write.'

'There is no hurry, you see. It will probably go on all my life and never be finished.'

Hudson threw the books back on the table. He talked for a time about the difficulty of making history readable without turning it into fiction. He was secretive about his manner of working, as if it was something to be ashamed of or some mystery that he had perfected himself and feared might be stolen from him. We talked for more than an hour. At last I got up to go.

'You know, I've enjoyed our jaw a lot,' Hudson said. He stopped and looked embarrassed.

'You must come and have a drink with me some time. Can I ring you up at your Territorials?'

'Of course.'

'I'll do that, then.'

'If I'm not there leave a message.'

There was something on his mind that he wanted to get out. He drew attention to one of the pictures as if he hoped to delay my going until he had come to some decision. At the head of the stairs he said:

'Look here, why don't you come and spend a week-end with my future in-laws, if you know them? I go down there once in a way, though of course I'm usually working over week-ends. Shall I tell them your address? I know they would like to see you again.'

'That would be very nice.'

'I'll do that, then. I'll tell them about you when I next see them.'

I thanked him and said good-night. The last suggestion was a little surprising. The Pimleys had probably forgotten ever having set eyes on me. But the following morning, certainly the following week-end, Hudson would hardly recall enough about the evening to cause an invitation to be sent. Even if it arrived it could always be declined unless the weather was good enough to make attractive the prospect of a visit to Camberley and a party of comparative strangers. If I thought at all about Hudson's words those were more or less my conclusions.

On the way home a poster outside a newspaper shop in a side street in Bayswater said:

FAMOUS TRAVELLER DIES SUDDENLY

It was about half-past ten in the morning and Bernard Judkins was crossing the square on his way from Charing

Cross. He had a house at Sevenoaks and came up every day. Watching him made one brood on the instinct for self-preservation with which he was so blessed. Though a resemblance existed, he was more heavily built than Hugh, with a grey moustache and a thick tuft of hair under his lower lip. Bernard had taken off his hat and was carrying it in his hand. His head was quite bald. He moved forward like a sleep-walker, glaring ahead and giving the impression that he might be run over at any moment. Somehow this never happened. Lorries, swinging round the square, stopped dead before they reached him. Boys on bicycles always swerved aside when an accident seemed inevitable. It was easy to see that there was a principle behind Bernard's methods. This was the way in which his life was ordered.

Reflections on these methods were interrupted by the buzzing of the house telephone. It was Hugh's voice. He said that he wanted to see me. He spoke with some agitation. This summons was already overdue. I set off down the stairs.

Hugh was sitting behind his writing-table arranging his pens and pencils in geometrical patterns. He looked thoroughly discomposed. Before I had time to shut the door behind me he said:

'You have seen about T. T. Waring, of course?'

'Yes.'

'It's rather dreadful.'

'Yes.'

'He was barely thirty.'

The papers had not been very informative about either the life or the death of T. T. Waring. It appeared that he had died of a chill in the south of France, probably at Sanary, as one account said that he had passed away in the Canaries. His age was variously given as 81 (clearly

36

a misprint for 31) to twenty-one, which would have meant that he had published his first book when he was about fourteen. The news came from Marseilles.

'I have already rung up Peppercorn,' Hugh said, 'and he tells me that all arrangements have been made for an eventuality of this sort. Royalties are to be paid into a trust fund to produce a T. T. Waring Memorial Edition in a suitable manner; the profits to go to the Society for the Encouragement of Oriental Travel and Research. Of course, living the life he did, he knew that this sort of thing might happen at any moment and provided accordingly.'

'Peppercorn?'

'No; T. T., of course.'

'It was clever of Mimi to know about it.'

Hugh frowned. He said:

'It is by no means certain when the news was published. I should need considerably more evidence than we were given before I believed that the medium's words had any reference whatever to T. T.'s death.'

'Are we going to bring out a life of him?'

'That,' said Hugh, 'is what I wanted to talk to you about. It must appear as soon as possible.'

The purpose of discussions such as the one in which Hugh and I were about to occupy ourselves was to provide Hugh with a sparring partner before he went in to Bernard to obtain his brother's consent to his schemes. On the whole, Hugh was not at all interested in what other people thought; though an occasional suggestion would sometimes strike him favourably and lie dormant for a time within him, to appear some weeks later as his own idea.

'That is obviously what we must do,' said Hugh; 'I thought of it at once. As soon as I got over the shock of the news.'

37

'I expect a lot of lives of T. T. Waring will appear. They will all be rushed out.'

Hugh was waiting for this. He wanted a dress rehearsal in preparation for Bernard's inevitable opposition. He said:

'We've got a new Waring manuscript coming in here anyway. I find that it arrived some weeks ago at Peppercorn's. Peppercorn has been laid up with 'flu and did not let us know about it. Anyone who writes the life will have to have access to this.'

'We had better see it first,' I said, in my capacity as understudy to Bernard.

'That manuscript will be all right,' said Hugh, in the voice he was going to use to clinch his argument.

The first round was over. Hugh had won. We sat back. Bernard was already more than half defeated.

'The question is,' said Hugh, 'who shall write the life? Here is a copy of the General List. You might like to run through it and mark suitable names.'

From among the oddments in front of him he took a small book bound in olive-green paper and held it out. I received it and glanced through the names.

'Redhead?'

'Redhead would ask too much money. Besides, we want him to finish what he is on at present.'

I turned over the pages. There seemed no one in the list capable of writing a saleable book of any sort, far less a satisfactory life of T. T. Waring.

'Mrs. Gulliver-Lawson?'

'I don't want a woman.'

'Mrs. Gulliver-Lawson has been everywhere and done everything. We bill her as that.'

'She wouldn't do at all.'

I came to the end of the catalogue and gave it back to

38

Hugh. His face showed that he had a candidate up his sleeve. For some reason he was unwilling to bring out the name at once. Hugh even looked a little ashamed of himself.

'I've had an idea,' he said. 'I don't know whether you will like it. It is a bit out of the way. But I think he will do it very well.'

Something ominous was coming.

'Who?'

'Handsworth.'

'*Shirley* Handsworth?'

'Yes,' said Hugh, going pink.

The suggestion was certainly startling. Hugh went on quickly:

'I know he has never tackled anything quite like this before. But I believe he would do it well. After all, his sales advance steadily.'

'It is hardly a T. T. Waring public, is it? We advertise T. T. Waring as a writer for Men.'

'All the more reason for getting him on the women's library lists. Besides, T. T. is read a lot by women too. That frontispiece of him in a turban—the silverpoint from a photograph that we collotyped—brought in appreciatory letters from women all over the country. And the colonies too.'

'We might have a photograph of each of them on the wrapper.'

Shirley Handsworth was another of Hugh's favourites. He did not, of course, come nearly as high up the lists as T. T. Waring, whose pre-eminence was unassailable. But he had a special line in boyishness that Hugh liked. T. T. Waring stood for the glorious extramundane ideal of Youth: Shirley Handsworth, for its grubby schoolboy reality. His sales, not large comparatively, were on the

39

increase. He found no difficulty in producing two, and sometimes three, books a year. These works were called historical reconstruction. They were serialised in papers for tired housewives. Bernard disliked Shirley as much as any author on the Judkins & Judkins list.

'And then,' said Hugh, 'Handsworth works so quickly. He'll have the thing ready in six months. And a long book too.'

'What will be thought next door?'

Hugh gave his snorting laugh. He said:

'I think there will be some antagonism certainly. But I'm going to try it.'

'At once?'

'Yes,' said Hugh. 'I wanted to sound you first. I am glad you agree with me. Handsworth said that he might be coming in this morning. I shall put up the suggestion at once. We can't afford to have any delay.'

Still wearing his skull-like grin, Hugh began to collect some of the books and papers that lay about on the table. After he had arranged these in a neat pile he waited for a few seconds, holding them while he listened for signs of life from Bernard's room. Then he stood up.

'Stay here,' he said.

He went out into the passage. I heard him knock on Bernard's door and go in.

The discussion on the further side of the partition began in a discreet murmur of grunts. It was unlikely that either of the brothers would succeed in maintaining this inaudible tone throughout its length. No more could be heard at this stage because at that moment a young man with black curly hair and full moist lips, set in a smile, burst into Hugh's office. He wore a loosely made camel's-hair overcoat, the unfastened belt of which trailed behind

40

him. When he saw that Hugh was not in the room he stopped short in the doorway.

'Hullo, Shirley.'

'Oh, where's Hugh? I thought I would come up without bothering to get them to announce me. Isn't he here?'

'He is next door with Bernard. He'll be back in a minute. How are you, Shirley? We were just talking about you.'

Shirley Handsworth sat down in Hugh's chair. The effort of all this scrambling up the stairs two steps at a time had been too much for him. He was short of breath. Now he looked sour and rather tired.

'What were you saying about me?' he said, not without suspicion.

'Only that we hoped there would be another book coming from you soon.'

Shirley looked as if he felt uncertain that this was the truth. He pouted.

'I came in to see whether the last one keeps up at all,' he said. 'They told me downstairs that Boots had a dozen last week.'

'Boots, Boots, Boots, Boots, moving up and down again?'

Shirley ignored this. He said:

'I thought Hugh might let me have some more money. I'm having an awfully expensive time just now. People never seem to leave one alone.'

'Shall I find out what the sales have been like the last few weeks?'

'Oh, do, my dear.'

'All right.'

I left Shirley to have a rummage through Hugh's letters and papers, which he began to do before I got out of the room. I went upstairs to the sales department to see how many of his last book we had managed to get rid of. It had been out for some months. The steady demand had

41

stopped, but recently there had been some orders for dozens and half-dozens which with an occasional single copy might by now have added up to a respectable number.

As usual, they took a long time to get out the figures. When I came back to Hugh's room I found Shirley, with one of Hugh's letters clasped in his hand, listening attentively at the keyhole of the folding-doors. The voices of Hugh and Bernard were raised in controversy. Hugh was saying:

'. . . but look here, he is too old and surely quite unsuitable. Why, I don't expect he has ever heard of him. If he has, he probably doesn't like the books at all. He is such an envious man too.'

'I don't know why you call him old,' Bernard's voice replied. 'He is younger than I am and can't be more than three or four years older than you, if that.'

Shirley turned to me.

'What are they talking about?' he said. 'Are they having a row? I can't make out what they are arguing about.'

'The affairs of the firm.'

'Yes, but what affairs?'

This was an undesirable situation. Either the partners should learn to modulate their voices or they should conduct their discussions in a sound-proof chamber. At any moment Shirley might hear his own name mentioned. Then the fat would be in the fire. However, Hugh and Bernard seemed to have passed the stage of arguing about Shirley. Presumably they were now debating some other candidate's qualifications for writing the T. T. Waring life. Now it was Hugh again. He sounded fairly angry.

'. . . Minhinnick is just the sort of person he makes fun of in his books. In fact, I don't see what possible reason we could have for commissioning him. He doesn't sell. We had to remainder his *Analysis of Fluctuations in the Copper*

Market and his *Silver is Gold*. We couldn't even do that
with *Aristogeiton: a Harmony*. We still have 1326 copies
of it that you won't allow me to pulp.'

Then came Bernard.

'Don't forget that Minhinnick spent a lot of his time in
the East as a young man. That would come in when dealing with the Oriental parts.'

Hugh's voice, shaking a little, as it always did when he
was angry, said:

'The East Minhinnick knew twenty-five years ago is not
the East of T. T. Besides, what does Minhinnick know of
the life of the youth of today? That is what gives the
Waring books their indefinable background. Besides,
Minhinnick has never been to Africa; nor America so
far as I know.'

'Perhaps not,' boomed Bernard. 'But he is a man of the
world.'

This was a status by which Bernard set great store. One
of the reasons why he had so resented the necessity for his
younger brother's intrusion into the business was his conviction that no schoolmaster could be a man of the world.
When Bernard said this he made such a noise that he must
have brought home to both of them that they could be
heard all over the square. He and Hugh now lowered
their voices. For a time there was only muttering. Shirley
lost interest. He began to tell a long story of how he had
just missed a contract to make a lecture tour in America.
In a few minutes we heard Bernard's door bang. Hugh
reappeared. Shirley jumped up with some of the romping
energy that had carried him up the stairs on his arrival.

'My dear Hughie, hullo.'

Hugh blushed. There was something about Shirley that
always caused him to blush when they met. Besides, it
always made him a little uncomfortable to be addressed as

'Hughie'. 'Hugh' was more usual. He countered with a great outburst of heartiness.

'Well, sir. And how are we?'

'Oh, Hughie, I came in to know if you could let me have a little more money. I'm terribly hard up. Absolutely stony-broke.'

Shirley put his head on one side and with his round, doggy eyes gazed at Hugh.

'Of course we shall have to see the figures.'

'I've got them here.'

Hugh took the paper on which were recorded the results of my visit to the sales department. I prepared to return to my room. As I opened the door to go out Hugh looked up quickly. He said:

'Don't go. I want you here about things.'

He sat looking at the paper in his hand, running his finger down the column of figures, smiling all the time to himself. He always showed signs of nervousness at the threat of being left alone with Shirley. Looking up at last, he said:

'Oh yes. I don't see why not. Say ten pounds.'

'Couldn't you make it twenty-five?'

Hugh seemed to consider for a second. Then he said:

'Yes, yes. Of course. If that is the amount you want. The main thing is for you to be contented.'

'Thank you awfully, Hugh. It is sweet of you.'

Hugh cleared his throat to show that the subject was dismissed for the time being.

'Shirley,' he said, 'did you ever read any of T. T. Waring's books?'

Shirley, whose face had brightened at the ease with which his financial needs had been satisfied, now became peevish again. He said:

'Oh, he's dead, isn't he? There was something about

44

it in the paper. I tried to read one of his books once. I thought it awful. I always thought all that mysteriousness so silly too. Of course I know I'm not a highbrow.'

Hugh pursed his lips and set his head a little at an angle as if the better to observe Shirley's tilted face. He said:

'T. T. Waring was not a highbrow, Shirley. There was nothing narrow about T. T. He wrote for all the world. Perhaps you did not give the book a fair chance. Some people found T. T. an acquired taste. I am sure you would have liked it if you had stuck to it, Shirley.'

'No. I'm sure I should never have liked it. It was the sort of thing I can't bear.'

Hugh made a hissing noise in his throat, expressing disagreement. Shirley tossed his head. He looked away from Hugh and out of the window at the trees of the square. Hugh tried another approach. It was clear that he diagnosed Shirley's attitude, no doubt rightly, as a simple case of jealousy.

'I've been thinking you ought to try a new line, Shirley,' he said. 'These historical reconstructions are all very well so far as they go. Of course they have sold excellently. That is all the more reason why the public should not be allowed to grow tired of them. What about a novel?'

Shirley showed some interest.

'You know, I can't write a novel, Hugh. I've tried. But you are right. I ought to give them something different next time. But what?'

Hugh nodded his head.

'We must think of something,' he said. 'I put up a suggestion this morning. But Bernard was against it.'

'Oh, that dreadful old man, even though he is your brother. How he hates me! What was it, Hughie?'

'Sssh. These walls are very thin. I am afraid I cannot possibly divulge a confidential conversation between two of

45

the firm's partners to satisfy even your curiosity, Shirley.'

'Give me some idea.'

'It was a suggestion that would surprise you, I think.'

Hugh sat back in his chair and folded his hands on the desk. His demeanour re-created vividly his schoolmastering days. You could almost see the blackboard behind him. I made another effort to escape. Again Hugh detained me.

'Something historical?' said Shirley.

'In a sense.'

'But I thought you wanted me to get away from all that sort of thing for a bit.'

'This was something rather different. Something that might bring into play the qualities that make the rest of your work a success. Of course you might not have liked the idea yourself. In fact, from something you said just now I am not at all sure that you would.'

'Do tell me, Hughie.'

Hugh shook his head. Shirley came round to the other side of Hugh's table, very close to Hugh. Looking down at him, Shirley repeated in a small humble voice:

'*Do* tell me what the suggestion was.'

Hugh laughed, fidgeted, and passed his hand over his reddish shreds of hair.

'I'll tell you what, Shirley,' he said. 'If you can guess it, I will reveal the secret to you. Not otherwise.'

'Oh, but, Hughie, how can I do that?'

Shirley retired to the chair again. He sat there looking reproachfully at Hugh. There was silence. Hugh shifted about uncomfortably, grinning all the time. Suddenly Shirley said:

'I believe it was something to do with T. T. Waring.'

The violence of the twitch that passed over Hugh's face unsettled his pince-nez.

'My dear Shirley, how did you guess?'

46

'I expect you wanted me to write his life or something.'
Hugh took a cigarette from the packet of Melachrino lying on the table. He offered them round. Shirley and I both refused. Hugh puffed out some little clouds of smoke, gasping to himself and chuckling.

'That was smart of you, Shirley,' he said. 'I must admit that was very smart.'

'And old Bernard didn't like the idea?'

Shirley was thoroughly roused now. Hugh must have seen this, but preferred not to lay all his cards at once on the table. He said:

'The way you talked about T. T. Waring when I mentioned his name first of all makes me think that my brother was probably right.'

Shirley stood up. He removed his camel's-hair overcoat. He hung it on a hook on the door and drew up a chair to the writing-table. Nonsense was at an end now. He wanted to talk business.

'Now look here, Hugh,' he said, 'I've guessed what it was. Now you must tell me the whole story. What did you suggest? What were Bernard's objections? Who does he want himself?'

Hugh squirmed about in his chair, showing his teeth. Shirley could be firm in matters of business.

'As soon as T. T. was dead,' Hugh said, '—that is, as soon as I got over the shock—I decided we must do a life of him. I thought over various possibilities. None of them seemed attractive. Then I thought, why not try someone completely new? In fact yourself. I suggested this to Bernard this morning. He did not seem to like the idea.'

'What did he say?'

'As you know, he always has a tendency to disagree. He showed few signs of wanting to publish a life of T. T. Waring at all. When I mentioned your name he would

47

not hear of it. However, I may succeed in talking him round if we decide that it would be a good thing for you to do.'

'But of course it would be a good thing for me to do. What an old drab he is! Who does he want to do it?'

Hugh cleared his throat again.

'Someone called Minhinnick,' he said.

'Who is he? I've never heard of him.'

'Minhinnick has written several books on economics. He also published an epic poem called *Aristogeiton*. He is one of the people Bernard has known for thirty or more years. He was a friend of my other brother, Paul, when he was alive. He contributes occasional articles to the weeklies.'

'Do his books sell?'

'They have what is called *succès d'estime*,' Hugh said guardedly.

'But why should he be pitched on to write a life of T. T. Waring?'

'Absolutely no reason whatever. I don't expect he has ever heard of T. T. Waring. It is just Bernard being difficult again. He wants to shelve the whole question.'

'But, Hugh, we mustn't let him do that.'

'No, no. Of course he can't be allowed to do that,' Hugh said.

All the same he did not look too hopeful.

'What do you think about it yourself?' he said. 'Do you think you could take it on if Bernard was squared?'

'But of course. It would sell awfully well. It would have all my publicity behind it and all T. T. Waring's as well.'

'It would entail a lot of trouble,' Hugh said, resuming his pedagogic drone. 'You realise that? It wouldn't be a thing you could just scribble off.'

'Now, Hughie, do you think that I ever just scribble things off, as you call it?'

48

'You have been very conscientious lately, I admit. I only said that because I was anxious for you to improve your sales with this.'

'Well, what are we to do?'

Hugh extinguished his cigarette. He altered the arrangement of the books lying on the table. He said:

'I think the best thing would be to wait for a day or two. You see, there are certain other difficulties here at the moment. They have got to be dealt with at the next Board meeting. I mentioned something of the sort to Bernard the other day. Possibly it is because of this that he is proving intractable.'

Shirley watched Hugh's face anxiously.

'Don't let the chance slip, Hughie,' he said. 'It might mean everything to my career.'

3

WHEN a letter directed to the office arrived from Mrs. Pimley, Captain Hudson's future mother-in-law, I had almost forgotten that he had promised that this should happen. Mrs. Pimley wrote that she had heard of my meeting with Hudson, and expressed a hope that I would stay with them the following week-end when we could renew our acquaintance. If this were possible Hudson would drive me there in his car. It would be nice to see me again and hear my gossip.

I could not flatter myself that most of the gossip I was in the position to recount would be of great interest to Mrs. Pimley; nor indeed would some of it be in the least suitable for her ears. However, before I had time to think things over, the telephone-bell rang. It was Hudson speaking from his orderly-room. He sounded a far more determined character than when he had emerged from the séance. I suddenly found that without a struggle I had agreed to visit the Pimleys. It was arranged that I should pick up Hudson at his flat after lunch on Saturday.

For the time being all was quiet on the T. T. Waring front. There had been a number of appreciations of his work in the literary papers. One or two dailies had had leaders about him. On the whole, there was less said than might have been expected. It appeared now that he had not died of a chill, as originally stated, but had been drowned while bathing. The earlier account had appeared first in an American paper. Sceptics suggested that he was not dead at all, but had arranged the whole thing as an incident in an advertising campaign, and that he would appear in several months with a book about some obscure spot to which he had travelled while the obituaries were appearing. Most people agreed with Hugh in thinking such a supposition not merely silly but also in the worst possible taste. Nothing further had been arranged about a biographer, but Hugh was preparing another attack. As a matter of fact, there was a lot to do at the office. Work in publishing comes in rushes. A ferment of manuscripts, delayed proofs, and bad-tempered authors occupied everyone's attention. Even Bernard found himself compelled to read and give his opinion on one or two books, so that the truce was voluntary on both sides.

I went round to Hudson at the end of the week. He had just finished strapping up a suitcase.

'Come on,' he said.

We set off for Camberley. The journey was not enjoyable. Hudson was morose and his car uncomfortable. He seemed to have lost all the friendliness he had shown at our previous meeting. I could not imagine why he had negotiated my invitation to stay with the Pimleys. When I saw more of him I found that he was often like this until he had been in one's company for an hour or so. A warming-up process had to take place.

'What did you think of Mimi drawing attention to the death of T. T. Waring the other night?'

'Mimi?' he said.

'At the séance. Don't you remember the medium kept on saying *"tee-tee"*?'

'Oh, that?' said Hudson. 'I thought it was a lot of rot.'

He was so gruff and uneasy that conversation was out of the question. We drove along in silence as far as the neighbourhood of Chobham Ridges. This sombre region of

pines and heather, an anonymous bit of country that might
have been anywhere in Europe, except for the character of
the English suburban architecture through which we
passed, woke him up. He said:

'When I retire I shan't settle here.'

'Nor me.'

'I say, I hope you won't be bored,' he said, 'there is nothing
whatever to do. Especially as you don't play golf. I wanted
you to meet Beryl again. Only—I never seem to have any
friends, so I thought she ought to see that I know somebody.'

He laughed as if he wanted to hide the embarrassment
he felt at making this speech.

'Perhaps my arrival will spread consternation.'

'Oh, rot!'

His face clouded. Not wanting him to sink back into his
earlier state of sulkiness, I hastily said:

'Have you known the Pimleys long?'

'I was at school with Alec,' Hudson said. 'That was how
I first got to know them. Then we didn't see each other
for years. The next thing was I met Beryl at the Derby.
We were one of a party who had chartered a bus to take
us there. It was frightfully wet. We got engaged soon after
that.'

'But who is Alec?'

'Beryl's brother.'

'I had no idea there was a son. What does he do?'

Huson laughed.

'They keep him pretty quiet,' he said. 'I don't think they
even know where he is now. He was a bad hat. He got
into a lot of ghastly messes in England, so they shipped him
off to the East. Then he got into a lot of ghastly messes
there. I don't think anyone knows where he is now. That
was all some time ago.'

'It must have been, because it is quite ten years since I knew them. I never heard him mentioned then.'

'It was about twelve or fifteen years ago,' Hudson said. 'Alec was a hopeless fellow. An absolute wrong 'un. Though not by any means a fool.'

'How did you come to be friends with him?'

'Well, you know how it is when you're at school. He seemed all right then. There was something rather attractive about him as a kid. He was always his grandfather's favourite.'

'There was a grandfather alive in those days, was there?'

'Alive in those days? He is alive now. Very much so.'

'I never met him.'

'Oh Lord,' said Hudson, 'I ought to have warned you about him. You see, he is over ninety and doesn't quite know what is going on. At least he is supposed not to. He sometimes comes out with some pretty telling remarks all the same.'

'Are there any other members of the family who will be new to me?'

'No. I think that is the lot,' Hudson said, laughing. 'The grandfather is called Captain Pimley, which seems all wrong when his son is a General.'

Soon after this we turned off the main road and drove along under pine trees. We passed some houses with white gates and short drives leading through laurel bushes.

'Here we are,' Hudson said.

The Pimleys' house was about three hundred yards from the road, set back a short way from a sandy lane which led to more pine woods and a common. It was the last of a row of similar detached red-brick, creeper-covered houses. Beyond it were clumps of gorse and bracken where Crown Land began. A man in shirt-sleeves whom I recognised as General Pimley was mowing the lawn. He was much as I remembered him, slight and wizened, with a dome-shaped head across the brow of which ran three heavily marked lines that gave him the worried humorous expression of an actor wearing a false forehead. When he saw us he hunched his shoulders and swung forward ape-like over the mower. His posture and the fact that he had removed his collar and tie heightened the illusion that he was a sad clown about to perform a tumbling act to entertain a not very appreciative audience.

I followed Hudson across the lawn and shook hands. General Pimley said a few words about the days when I had known them on Salisbury Plain, enquired after my family, asked if I still collected stamps; and seemed relieved to hear that I did not play golf. He said:

'In that case you won't mind if Tiger and I fit in nine holes between tea and dinner.'

Hudson was evidently a favourite with his prospective father-in-law. While we were talking Beryl came out of the house. She kissed Hudson, and turning to me said how glad she was that he and I had met. Time had improved her. She was fair, with a slight tendency to freckles. The pointedness of her features, even a kind of foxiness, was not unattractive. Hudson had told me she was twenty-nine. Like so many girls whose lot has been to lead dull lives, her manner implied that all men were her slaves. Hudson naturally figured as her most notable vassal. She was clearly proud of having captured him.

We walked towards the house. The General, putting on his collar as he went, said:

'Has your grandfather had his tea yet?'

'He is on his way up now,' Beryl said.

We passed through a small conservatory into an inner hall filled with heavy furniture and Indian ornaments made of silver. Here progress was delayed by some dis-

54

lodgment that was taking place. The light was dim. At first I could not see what was happening. A group of figures were moving slowly away from us, swaying a little as they went. These persons assumed the forms of Mrs. Pimley, unchanged from the days of Salisbury Plain, a maid, and a very old man, who appeared to be in process of transference from one room to another. When he saw Hudson the old man withdrew his arm from one of his supporters. He held out his shaking hand. At the same time he opened his mouth but did not speak.

'That's Tiger,' said Mrs. Pimley, who had not yet seen me standing in the background with Beryl. 'Tiger has just arrived from London. Doesn't he look well?'

'How are you, sir?' said Hudson. 'We've had a pretty good run down from town. I hope you got over that cold you were suffering from when I last stayed here.'

I admired the way he took the situation in hand. It was strange that anyone who found so many ordinary social relations embarrassing should be able to convey such a feeling of ease at this moment. He touched the old man's arm. Captain Pimley, who had a wispy grey moustache that curled down over his upper lip in the direction of his mouth, gazed abstractedly at Hudson.

'Come along,' said Mrs. Pimley, again taking the arm—and then, catching sight of me lurking in the shadows, she added:

'Oh, how do you do. I never saw you. How rude of me. Do forgive me while I arrange about my father-in-law's rest. I am so looking forward to a talk with you about everything.'

At the sound of my voice replying to this speech Captain Pimley turned from Hudson. He tried to take a step forward and held out a trembling finger in my direction. Then he said:

55

'Al . . . ec. . . .'

There was silence for a few seconds. I muttered some acknowledgment of this greeting. Mrs. Pimley said:

'Come along, then.'

The cortège moved forward up the stairs. The rest of us entered the drawing-room. Winefred was sitting on the sofa, reading a book.

This was inevitably a set-piece. Winefred must have heard our arrival. She continued to read for about half a minute after we came through the door. Then, looking up with all the appearance of surprise, she laid down the book and held out her hand. Unlike Beryl, she showed no improvement. She was all teeth and badly cut brown hair. Her appearance might have been remedied, because she had rather large grey eyes and firm eyebrows, but Winefred by her manner made matters worse. Her approach was threatening. She showed no signs of wishing to make friends. She merely said: 'Nice to see you after all these years,' and, turning at once to Hudson, went on:

'You're earlier than usual, aren't you?'

'Perhaps a shade,' he said. 'I've got a new car.'

'I wondered how much longer that old Morris would last.'

'Tiger has got rid of it now,' Beryl said. 'I told you. He got ten pounds.'

Winefred closed her book. She peered forward as if the subject was of the utmost interest to her. Addressing herself to Beryl as if Hudson himself were not present, she said:

'And has he really got a new one?'

'I've got a new second-hand one,' said Hudson. He spoke as if he resented Winefred's manner.

'Oh, I see.'

While this conversation had been taking place General

56

Pimley had been completing his toilet in front of a small mirror that hung above a secretaire. He finished buttoning up his waistcoat and said:

'Come upstairs and I'll show you your room. Tiger has his usual quarters.'

He led the way to a small room which appeared to be his own dressing-room. A great many pairs of highly polished boots and shoes stood round the floor, and photographs of regimental groups hung on the walls. General Pimley pointed to one of these. He said:

'One of that beauty chorus was me when I was at the Shop. A prize of sixpence is offered to any guest who guesses which one. You have the whole week-end to think it over. Bathroom right and right again.'

He shut the door. I was left alone to examine the situation. The room was at the side of the house and the view from the window was agreeable. No houses were to be seen. There was a stretch of rough grass beyond the garden and one or two trees that were not conifers. While I was considering this prospect there was a knock on the door. Hudson came in. He sat down in a rocking-chair that stood in the corner of the room.

'I say, I hope you weren't horrified by all that business in the hall,' he said. 'Are you sure you never met the grandfather when you knew them before?'

'I seem to remember seeing the family at a horse-show once with an old man in tow. I'm not certain whether it was him.'

'He didn't live with them permanently in those days. He has to be looked after now, of course. Do you know, he first went out to India with a commission in the Honourable East India Company's army. Takes you back a bit, doesn't it?'

'You seem to get along with him all right.'

'Oh well,' said Hudson modestly, 'you know the old boy has quite a spot of money that is very difficult to get out of him. He is supposed to be coughing up a bit when Beryl and I get married. But even that is uncertain.'

'Why did he call me Alec?'

'I suppose he somehow jumped back to the time he first met me: when I was brought over by Alec when we were at school together. I wish he wouldn't do that sort of thing. How do you find the rest of the family?'

'Beryl is prettier than ever. The parents and Winefred haven't changed much. The General looks a shade older.'

'I don't know what is wrong with Winefred,' Hudson said. 'I suppose she wants a man. I don't mind people being rude to me. What I can't stand is this sort of la-di-da nonsense we all have to put up with from her.'

'Perhaps she will grow out of it.'

'She'll have to be damned quick,' Hudson said. 'She is twenty-eight. Shall we go down?'

Mrs. Pimley, having disposed of her father-in-law satisfactorily, had returned to the drawing-room. She was a talkative woman with neat grey hair and a good nose and forehead. She began asking all sorts of questions as to what I was doing and where I was living, at the same time describing all the places she herself had visited since we had last met. Tea was brought in. Only then did Winefred put down her book and move from the sofa to a chair near the tea-table.

'What is the book you are so engrossed in?' I said.

'It's an old one of T. T. Waring's. I've read it before. I thought I would read it again.'

'He must be a stout fellow, that young man,' General Pimley said. 'I picked that book up and read a few pages of it the other day. That mountain-trip of his sounded a

58

pretty good show. Weren't you saying something about him, Tiger?'

'Only that I enjoyed his books very much,' Hudson said. 'He is dead now, you know. He died the other day. You have the honour of having his publisher to stay in the house.'

'Oh, are you?' said Mrs. Pimley. 'How extraordinarily interesting that must be.'

'You don't mean to say you have taken to liking the books Winefred reads, have you, Father?' said Beryl.

'I liked that one,' said the General.

However, he did not seem disposed to embark on a literary discussion.

'I suppose, Beryl, you have never heard of T. T. Waring?' Winefred said.

'Don't be absurd. I always thought he looked rather attractive in his pictures. If he didn't wear such awful clothes.'

'What's wrong with his clothes?'

'All those turbans and things.'

'They are the proper clothes to wear in the East,' said Winefred. 'I suppose you have never read any of his books.'

'I have. I read the one about the island.'

'Then why did you think it funny that Father should like what I was reading?'

'Only because he doesn't usually like your books. Neither do I.'

'But is he really dead?' said Mrs. Pimley. 'I read that one he wrote about the long walk he did in Asia. I enjoyed it very much.'

'You know, I am awfully interested in that fellow for some reason,' said Hudson. 'I like the way he describes what he has done. It isn't just a bare narrative like most travellers. It makes you think.'

'You'd better write his life,' I said. 'There seem to be difficulties about the present candidate for the job.'

'By Jove, that would be an interesting job,' Hudson said. 'I wish I could.'

After tea Hudson and General Pimley had their game of golf. Mrs. Pimley suggested a walk. She and Beryl and I went up through the pines and strolled for a time on the common. Winefred disappeared somewhere on her own. While we were waiting for Mrs. Pimley to put on a hat Beryl said:

'It's rather a shame that Father should drag Tiger off to play golf as soon as he arrives. After all, I don't see him as often as all that.'

The violence with which she said this was unexpected. She had shown no sign of sulkiness in front of Hudson. The way she spoke made me think that she must be very much in love with him.

On Sunday morning the weather was showery. Mrs. Pimley came into the drawing-room where we were all sitting reading the papers after breakfast. She was dressed for church, but appeared to expect no one to accompany her. She said to her husband:

'Are you going in to get the car, Tom? We shall want it this afternoon. Why don't you walk into the town with me and drive it back? They promised it should be ready yesterday evening. We forgot to fetch it.'

General Pimley continued to read the *Observer* for some moments. Then he removed his spectacles, sighed, and went upstairs. A few minutes later he and his wife, dressed in burberries, crunched past the window. They walked with determination.

'What are we all going to do?' Beryl said.

She and Hudson were sitting on the sofa with a picture paper between them. Winefred said:

'I am going to tend my garden.'

'Do you have your own special one?' I asked.

'Just a few bulbs. Quite silly.'

'May I see it?'

'There is nothing to see. No, really. I just amuse myself with it. If one lives in the country one must have interests like that.'

'But I should like to see it.'

'No, no,' said Winefred, smiling horribly.

She stood up quickly and went out of the room. Hudson stretched. He said:

'That sister of yours needs something drastic done to her.'

'How shall we amuse ourselves?' Beryl said. She showed no interest in the problem of Winefred.

I said that I thought of going for a walk.

'What energy,' said Hudson.

Presumably they wanted to be left alone. There were plans of some sort for the afternoon, and, as space was somewhat restricted in the house, an hour or so to oneself was something to be grateful for. Neither of them suggested coming too.

I went upstairs to get a mackintosh. When I came down again and approached the front door a cloudburst was in progress. There was no reason to go out in this. At the same time, to return to the drawing-room might disturb Hudson and Beryl. I went into a room the door of which stood half open. It was a sort of smoking-room. I was examining the pictures there, coloured prints of the cities of India in the 'forties, when a voice said:

'Is it still . . . raining?'

Captain Pimley was sitting in front of the fire, concealed

by the back of his arm-chair. He had a rug round his knees. A bell stood beside him on a neighbouring table in case any crisis should arise.

'I think it is only a shower.'

'What is your . . . name?'

I told him. I added that I was a friend of Hudson, who had brought me down with him the day before. The old man said:

'I remember . . . now.'

'But I am afraid I am disturbing you. I was going out for a walk when the rain began. I came in here for a minute or two until it stopped.'

'Where is Beryl and her . . . her . . . her . . .'

'They are in the drawing-room.'

Captain Pimley laughed. He said:

'So they are in the . . . drawing-room, are . . . they?"

'Yes.'

I laughed too, but did not manage to catch the spontaneous jocularity that Captain Pimley seemed to feel about the matter. The rain was still thudding against the window-pane, so that at the moment there was no chance of escape. Captain Pimley said:

'I thought you were my grand . . . son Al . . . ec.'

'Am I like him?'

'What's that?'

'Do I look like your grandson Alec?'

'No.'

He brought out this with considerable emphasis. Conversation came to a temporary standstill. Then he began again:

'My grand . . . son Al . . . ec.'

'Yes?'

'. . . is a scoundrel.'

'Is he?'

'He is a tre . . . mendous scoundrel,' said Captain Pimley.
'He lives abroad, doesn't he?'
'What?'
'He doesn't live in England?'
'Who?'
'Alec.'
'What about him?'
'Does he live in England?'
'Certainly not.'

Captain Pimley rose from the chair after saying this. With the rug still draped round his knees and held in place by one hand, he hobbled slowly across the room and out of the door. It seemed a good opportunity to leave as the rain had to some extent abated. I got out of the house without delay, ignoring the few drops that continued to fall for the next ten minutes.

The common where we had walked the previous evening was a deserted tract of land, typical of Surrey, looking as if it might be miles from any habitation, while only a few deciduous trees divided it from country studded with bungalows. Some of the land showed traces of heath fires, charred roots and stones lying about on the blackened ground. Walking there was not at all like being in the country. Agriculture seemed as remote as in a London street. This waste land might have been some walled-in space in the suburbs where business men practised golf-strokes; or the corner of a cinema studio used for shooting wilderness scenes. It had neither memories of the past nor hope for the future.

For a time I tramped along. At one moment the rain began to threaten again, but the clouds cleared before I turned back. Coming home by a different route from that which I had taken on the way out, I found a small gate leading into the back of the Pimleys' garden. This seemed the best way to return to the house. The gate had a high hedge on either side of it. I was shutting it behind me when someone passed quickly round the farther side of the hedge and pushed by. There was the impression of a vaguely Oriental presence, flannel trousers, and a dark visage: something that recalled Indian students pattering about Bloomsbury. For a moment I wondered whether I had been mistaken or whether the Pimleys had a gardener of Asiatic origin. I turned round to see what the back view looked like. The figure had disappeared into the ground.

Further on in the garden Winefred was standing by a tree, occupied apparently with her thoughts. When I spoke to her she jumped as if she had been stung by a wasp.

'Who was the dusky stranger?'

'What do you mean?'

'Didn't I pass a coloured gentleman on the way back from my walk?'

'I have no idea where you have been walking.'

Her manner was not encouraging.

'I just came through your back gate. I thought I saw a man as black as night.'

'Nonsense,' she said, 'it was the gardener. I expect he had been cleaning out the flue in the stoke-hole.'

As we went together towards the house General Pimley came towards us from the other side of the lawn.

'I've got the car,' he said. 'She seems all right now. We shall be able to use her this afternoon.'

'Is the house we are going to far?'

'No,' he said. 'A mile or two. Do you know this part of the country?'

'We lived near here for a bit when I was a child.'

'You know,' said General Pimley, 'they say a soldier can see all the salient points of his career from a piece of high

64

ground in this neighbourhood: Wellington—Sandhurst—The Staff College—Broadmoor.'

I laughed. Winefred made no effort to relax her features. No doubt she had heard it before. That did not excuse her. It was no wonder that General Pimley looked worn with such a daughter. He said:

'So you don't keep up your stamp collection any longer? When you were a boy you were very keen on it.'

'I remember you took an interest in it that flattered me very much. I haven't looked at it for years. I'm always meaning to sell it. I suppose it is worth something now. You showed me your stamps. Do you still go on?'

'Certainly I do. Only line-engraved, of course. I've been branching out lately. I've left the British Empire.'

'Where have you gone to?'

'United States before 1870.'

'But that was what I used to specialise in.'

'Did you?' said General Pimley. 'I'd forgotten that. And you still have the collection?'

'It's knocking about somewhere.'

'Why not let me have a look at it some time?'

'I should be delighted to if it would amuse you.'

'We might even do a deal.'

'There is nothing I should like better.'

'Good heavens,' said Hudson, who had come up and stood listening to this conversation, 'are you a philatelist?'

'I used to be.'

'It's nothing to be ashamed of, Tiger,' said General Pimley. 'It would teach a young fellow like you some geography if you took an interest in stamps. More than you'll ever learn from T. T. Waring or whatever his name is.'

Soon after that the gong sounded for lunch.

·   ·   ·   ·   ·   ·

65

Nothing of interest happened during the remainder of the week-end. In the afternoon we played tennis with some of the Pimleys' friends. After dinner Hudson motored me back to London. It was a fine night and we got up in good time.

'I hope you weren't too bored,' Hudson said as we were saying good-night.

'Not a bit.'

'It was fine talking to the General about his stamps. They are the only thing he really takes any interest in.'

'It was amusing seeing all the Pimleys again.'

'What did you think of Beryl?'

'Charming.'

It was a fearful word, and the last one to describe the qualities Beryl possessed. On the spur of the moment I could think of no other. Hudson pondered over it.

'Yes,' he said, as if the idea had only just struck him, 'she is charming, isn't she? Well, we must meet again soon.'

On Monday morning tnere was a message by telephone at the office to say that Hugh would be away that day, and probably for the day or two following, on account of a chill he had caught over the week-end. Hugh was always having trouble with his inside. His own remedies combined a lot of fussing (he once admitted to me that as a young man he had worn goloshes) with bouts of imprudence such as discarding his thick underclothes at the first sign of spring. This also I had on his own authority and saw no reason to disbelieve.

Work was held up when Hugh was absent, for, although Bernard put up a show of disagreeing with Hugh's decisions, on matters of importance he was unwilling to make any of his own. Sometimes he modified orders that

66

Hugh had given. This was usually to cause petty annoyance rather than to indicate a change of policy. When Bernard sent for me that afternoon I supposed that some such intention was in his mind and that he wanted to ascertain how far it would be safe to go in his system of Hugh-baiting. It was unusual for him to express a wish to see anyone in the afternoon, which he was accustomed to spend in a state of comatose disapproval of modern life.

Bernard's desk was at right angles to the window. Behind it he had made a nest for himself, a refuge against the world, where he could recapture same vestiges of pre-natal irresponsibility. A broad parapet of books stretched across the top of the desk. Another similar but higher barrier ran along the ledge of the window, so that he could neither see out of it nor be seen from the square. The shelves of another bookcase at his back tipped forward waywardly as if at any moment they might void their contents on his head. His fourth and most vulnerable side was protected by newspapers thrown about on the floor in such quantities that they formed a sort of pyramid. When visitors ignored this barricade Bernard would point warningly to the ground as if these journals concealed chasms yawning in the floor. Everything round him was covered with dust. A faint reminiscence of stale vegetables hung about the room, generated by old books and cigar-smoke. Signed photographs of authors hung on every available space on the walls. Most of these went back to the time of Eli Judkins, the founder of the firm. There was nothing dated later than 1917.

Bernard was not alone. A square-looking elderly man with a lot of white hair trimmed on Roundhead principles was sitting in front of the fireplace. He wore a thick gentleman-farmer sort of suit. On the table beside him lay a broad-brimmed black hat and a gnarled walking-stick. I recognised Minhinnick. Throned in the tattered armchair he looked every inch an unsuccessful literary man. Bernard, who had given Minhinnick one of his cigars, mumbled something about our having met before. Minhinnick's façade was far from friendly; but he held out his hand. It had been my duty to put before him the facts with regard to the small sale enjoyed by *Aristogeiton: a Harmony*. He must have known intuitively that I belonged to the faction that favoured pulping.

Bernard, who wore a collar made of a single band of starched linen that went rather more than once round his neck and was itself encircled by a silk tie passed through a ring, pressed the stub of his cigar into an ash-tray. He removed his spectacles and managed to look quite genial. The grey moustache and the tuft of hair under his lower lip bristled forward.

'We were having a talk about T. T. Waring,' he said.

This was a portentous bit of information. It could only mean that Bernard was taking the opportunity of Hugh's absence to get in his own candidate to write the biography. There would be a serious row when Hugh heard of this. So far as I knew, there was no reason why Bernard should care tuppence who wrote the book. At the same time Minhinnick was an old friend, possibly in need of money. This might be a deliberately violent move to force Hugh's hand in some more important matter. Bernard, realising that his words could not fail to sound a minatory note, added:

'Hugh and I had a chat about the question. We weren't able to arrive at a decision.'

I bowed my head. Bernard was putting on an act for me to describe to Hugh. He turned to Minhinnick and with unnatural articulation, as if speaking to a foreigner, said:

'You were telling me how interested you were in T. T. Waring, were you not, Minhinnick?'

Minhinnick rubbed his leg. He began to make a low wheezing, as if getting up steam. At last the words came from deep down within him:

'I was saying that I wondered whether he was any relation to the Waring who wrote *Fabian Days and Fabian Ways*. I used to know him before he went under, poor fellow. Or whether this man was descended from Bishop Waring of the sermons.'

'Of course that would have to be established,' Bernard said encouragingly.

'I should not be at all unwilling to go into such matters,' said Minhinnick. 'After all, I have travelled extensively. My name is by no means unknown to the critics.'

Bernard turned to me as if he expected comment of some sort. I bowed again. Minhinnick's name was known to the critics all right. The question was whether he had ever read a line written by T. T. Waring. I doubted this. But Minhinnick had got started. He said:

'It seems to me far from desirable that the task of biography should be entrusted to someone too fulsome— some mere eulogist. That is not at all what is required.'

'No, no,' said Bernard, 'nobody wants that.'

'What is needed,' said Minhinnick, 'is an honest estimate of the young man's qualities. Neither more nor less.'

'You just want to be fair,' said Bernard.

Even now no one had said in so many words that Minhinnick would be a good person to write the life. These two might drone on for hours without ever coming out in the open about this. On the other hand, once he and Minhinnick and I had discussed the matter in conclave

Bernard would gain a certain moral force when it came to dealing with Hugh. To act in this way was practically a declaration of open war against Hugh on Bernard's part. As Hugh's hired assassin I did not want to be drawn in on the wrong side. To mention Shirley Handsworth's name as Hugh's candidate would give Hugh away.

'I rather understood from Hugh that he had someone in mind.'

Bernard was ruthless. He swept the words aside.

'I know,' he said.

This was certainly acting tough.

'My brother is a strange fellow,' said Bernard, speaking with terrible bonhomie. 'Once he gets a thing into his head nothing on earth will get it out.'

'Who does he want to do it?' Minhinnick said.

This was impertinence. It was the sort of thing a publisher might just stand from an author who sold ten or twenty thousand copies. From an old hack like Minhinnick who had difficulty in getting even friends to publish his books it was a bit more than even Bernard would take. So at least I thought. I was wrong. Bernard not only kept his temper, he actually gave the information.

'Shirley Handsworth,' he said.

'Shirley Handsworth?'

It showed the state that Minhinnick must have reached that he should be prepared to admit that he had heard of someone like Shirley. Even if he did not choose to keep up appearances in front of Bernard he might be expected to do so when a subordinate member of the firm was present. He said:

'Your brother must be crazy.'

'I reasoned with him,' said Bernard, 'but he was very insistent. Of course I know that some of Handsworth's

70

historical reconstructions have done well. The one about the queen, whatever her name was, who slept with all her ministers'—Bernard in his capacity of man-of-the-world brought this out with a grunt and a low chuckle—'was quite a success in a small way. But what ever has that got to do with it?'

There was something to be said for this view. I preferred to identify myself with neither faction. As a matter of fact I wanted to get back to some notes I was making on Stendhal's *Journals*.

'Handsworth's name would spell disaster in a work of that sort,' Minhinnick said. 'Disaster and worse.'

He did not enlarge on such a prospect. But he was sufficiently carried away by his feelings to reveal that Bernard had made an offer by saying:

'I see no reason why I should not write the life of this young traveller as you were flattering enough to suggest. It seems to me that the best thing would be for me to send along a few of my qualifications, literary and otherwise, for undertaking the biography. It is always better to have something on paper.'

Bernard would no doubt have preferred the matter of himself having suggested this to have been stated a little less definitely. At that moment a message came to say that I was wanted downstairs. It turned out that a report had been returned accidentally to an aspirant author with his manuscript. This had upset him so much that he had come round to see us about it. An explanation took some time. When I returned to Bernard's room Minhinnick had departed. He had probably been sent away by Bernard as soon as possible. Bernard had done all he wished for his purpose. Minhinnick's claim had been staked out as a rival to Shirley's. Bernard showed no sign of wishing to discuss the question further. He glanced up from the copy of the *Illustrated Sporting and Dramatic* which lay in front of him. His face puckered like that of a bad-tempered baby. The little scut of yellow cotton-wool under his lower lip stuck out resentfully. I withdrew.

4

WHEN Roberta Payne turned up at a party given by some people called Manasses, we had not met since the Fitzgibbon wedding. Roberta was not so brown as she had been on that occasion, but some connoisseurs considered that sunburn did not suit her and that she looked her best when pale and tired. As soon as she saw me she said:

'When are you going to bring out a life of T. T. Waring?'

'It is due in the near future. I am glad there is already a public demand for it.'

Roberta looked what she herself was accustomed to call 'awfully mysterious'.

'Naturally *I* am interested,' she said.

Hugh had returned to the office in a bad temper after his chill. It had not been long before he heard about Bernard's negotiations with Minhinnick. During the words that followed Bernard had laid down that he would in no circumstances consider Shirley Handsworth's name as a possible writer of the T. T. Waring biography. Hugh was equally firm that the book should not be written by Minhinnick. This sort of dispute had taken place before between the brothers, but the need to publish the life as soon as possible made the deadlock more serious than usual. When he had cooled down, Hugh had shown signs of distress at his handling of the situation. It looked as if the book would be postponed indefinitely. However, there was no reason to tell this to Roberta.

'Why should you be specially interested in T. T. Waring?'

'I was engaged to him, as a matter of fact.'

I did not believe a word of this; but it was such an amusing idea that it deserved encouragement.

'But how dreadful for you that this should have happened. When were you due to get married?'

'The engagement was broken off.'

'None of us heard anything about it.'

'You know what he was like. Did you never meet him?'

'No.'

'I thought not. Otherwise you would not have asked that. He had this almost pathological desire for secrecy.'

'When was this?'

'In France about eighteen months ago.'

'You could be of great help to the biographer when we find him.'

'That was what I wanted to talk to you about. Is Shirley Handsworth going to do it?'

'I don't know. His name was mentioned.'

'Or Minhinnick?'

'How well informed you always are, Roberta. Really it isn't decided yet. You probably know much more about it than I do.'

'I think they are both too *mesquin* for words.'

'So do I.'

It would be fun if Roberta were to write the book herself. But they did not want a female author for the job. Besides, it was possible that Roberta would lack the energy necessary to write even the worst book of the required length. Clearly she thought there was money to be made out of the situation. Roberta was not a girl who believed in giving something for nothing.

'Can't you get hold of someone better than those two

74

horrors?' she said. 'You see, I might be able to supply you with some quite useful stuff.'

'Why not come round and see Hugh Judkins about it some time? Have you met him?'

'Never. What is he like?'

'Rather shy. I think you are his type.'

'I like shy men.' said Roberta. 'But hadn't I better tell you what happened first? Then you can advise me as to the best way of presenting my story to Mr. Judkins.'

'What about finding some chairs?'

We went through into another room where there was less noise. Roberta sat down on an Empire settee terminating in gilt swans, and put her feet up. I took the music-stool.

'I was staying with friends,' Roberta said, 'in a villa not far from Toulon.'

'Anyone I know?'

'I don't think so. Anyway, I took the car into the town to buy some things one day. When I came out of the shop I found I had parked in the wrong place or driven up a one-way street or something. There was a policeman there. I tried to explain what had happened, but he talked such *méridional* French that we couldn't understand each other.'

Roberta's eyes began to expand at the memory of the incident as if she were again trying to quell the Provençal gendarme.

'Then a man saw the G.B. on the car. He came up and asked if I were English. He got the whole thing fixed up in two seconds.'

'And this was T. T. Waring?'

'I didn't find that out until much later.'

'What was he like?'

'Dark, and I thought rather—well, not exactly good-looking—but interesting.'

75

'How was he dressed?'

'The usual south of France things. Workman's trousers and a sports shirt.'

'Not a burnous or a djibbah?'

'Don't be absurd. Anyway, he told me he had an *appartement* on the Vieux Port. He made me promise to come and see him. He seemed interested in where I was staying and admired the car a lot.'

'What sort of a car was it?'

'Rather a nice Hispano, as a matter of fact. I didn't bother to tell him it wasn't my own.'

'When did you find out he was T. T. Waring?"

'Don't be so impatient. He was rather secretive about his real name. He said: "I am always known here as Robinson. It is a name the French like so much, and really it is as good as any other." '

'Wasn't that rather odd?'

'You know what one's friends are. Anyway, I used to go and see him. I should add that it was all frightfully respectable.'

'And then one day he proposed?'

'Well, to tell the truth I was getting a tiny bit bored with him. You see, there were certain reasons why I could not very well ask him to come and see me at the villa, so I told him that I lived there with my grandmother, who was rather eccentric and ill and did not like young men coming to the house.'

'What did he say to that?'

'He asked me if she was going to leave me the villa when she died. I said she was. I'm afraid I told him an awful lot of lies. He was so inquisitive, and it always seemed to please him so much when I pretended to have good prospects.'

'Was he still Mr. Robinson to you?'

76

'Of course. Then one day I was having tea in his flat and he left me alone while he went out to get some brioches. I was looking round the room and saw a brown-paper parcel. There wasn't any string round it and I looked inside.'

'Weren't you afraid that Mr. Robinson would come back and catch you?'

'The paper was loosely folded over a typewritten manu-script. I only lifted up one side of it. There wasn't any undoing to be negotiated.'

'I see.'

'There was a letter pinned to the first page of the typing. It was to Peppercorn, the literary agent. It had various instructions about the new T. T. Waring travel book, which was what the manuscript inside the parcel turned out to be.'

'Well?'

'One of the things the letter said was that until further notice Peppercorn was to address all communications to Monsieur Robinson at the flat on the Vieux Port.'

'But perhaps Robinson was another agent of T. T. Waring.'

'The letter was in the same writing as several notes that Robinson had sent me. It was signed T. T. Waring.'

'In fact, calling himself Robinson in France was one of T. T. Waring's many peculiarities.'

'I saw at once that that was who he must be.'

'What was the next step?'

'He came back with the brioches and we had tea. When the meal was over he suddenly began a long speech about vagrom men and rolling stones and a woman's touch—which all ended up with his asking me to marry him.'

'Were you surprised?'

'My dear, I was paralysed. You see, there had never been

the slightest question of his making love to me. To tell you the truth, I thought he had other interests.'

'And you accepted him?'

'I was rather prim and said I should have to think it over. You see, I don't like to be cynical, but it was quite clear that he thought I was very rich. I didn't want the poor dear to have too much of a shock when he found out the truth.'

'Did you tell him that you knew he was T. T. Waring?'

'At first I could not make up my mind whether I ought to or not. You see, if he really wanted to marry me it was up to him to warn me about a thing of that sort. Besides, I thought it would anyway be quite good publicity to be engaged to him for a time. After all, one has to think about that sort of *réclame* if one wants to sell one's articles. If I told him that I knew who he was I thought he might get angry and break the whole thing off.'

'So what happened?'

'In the end I admitted that I had discovered he was T. T. Waring. At first he denied it. Then he got in a fearful state and made me promise never to breathe a word to a soul. He said that he had offended a secret society in China by something he had written and that if they knew where he was they would send someone to murder him, with ghastly tortures beforehand.'

'Did you believe that?'

'I didn't, really.'

'And then you broke it off?'

'This is what happened. Strictly against my orders he came over to see me one day at the villa where I was staying. Of course he quite misunderstood the whole situation. I mean, I suppose he guessed that I really had no money. I'm sure he thought the most awful things about me too.'

'How unpleasant he sounds.'

'Anyway, I never saw him again. There was no point in my telling anyone about the broken engagement. It would only have meant that he would have said all sorts of horrid and untrue things about me. Now he is dead, of course things are different.'

There was a pause during which Roberta fingered her diamond wrist-watch, a souvenir possibly of the 'friends' with whom she had stayed at the villa. She said:

'I don't think I had better tell Mr. Judkins the story as I have told it to you. What do you think?'

'He might hear a slightly more idealised version. T. T. Waring is one of his heroes.'

'He was one of mine until that happened,' said Roberta. 'Look, I'm rather busy this week. I will come in and see you in a few days' time. You can introduce me. Then we can talk things over.'

'How are your memoirs getting on?'

'The death of T. T. has rather changed the situation as regards them,' Roberta said. 'But I'm awfully hungry. Shall we try and find something to eat? I think I saw some caviare.'

The next day a series of disasters took place at the office. News arrived of the liquidation of an important North Country bookseller who had just received a large consignment of Judkins & Judkins' stock; Redhead's manuscript came in 30,000 words too short and entitled *Than Whom What Other*; the telephone was out of order from eleven o'clock to three-thirty-five; and the office boy gave notice because he said that one of the invoice clerks was 'always on at him'. It was no wonder that Hugh was worried.

'We must fix up something about the T. T. Waring life,' he said, 'we really must. Surely you can think of some other possible writers. You ought to be in touch with the younger people.'

This seemed a good moment to make a suggestion.

'Do you remember Captain Hudson? The soldier we met at Mrs. Cromwell's house. He walked some of the way home with us.'

'Rather a personable young man?'

'Personable' was one of Hugh's highest terms of praise. It was a hopeful sign that he should use it of Hudson.

'He is very keen on T. T. Waring's work. He writes competently. I have seen some of his stuff. Why not get him to do it?'

Hugh became suspicious at once.

'Oh no,' he said. 'I do not think that would do at all.'

This was a matter of routine. Nothing would have beer more disturbing than instant acceptance of the scheme on Hugh's part. Besides, it was a most revolutionary suggestion. The idea of this as a serious business proposition had come to me when pondering on Roberta's revelations about T. T. Waring. If she could get engaged to him, Hudson might be able to write his life. After a short silence Hugh said:

'You mean that Bernard might consider someone whom none of us really know anything about?'

'Exactly.'

'Have you any real reason to suppose that this man could do it?'

'He is immensely interested in T. T. Waring. And obviously industrious.'

'What have you seen that he has written?'

'Some pages of a regimental history.'

'That is hardly the sort of thing one can judge from.'

There was another pause. Hugh fidgeted with the things on his table. At last he said:

'But would he have the time to do it?'

'That I can't say. He has all the books at his finger-tips. It depends on what additional material there is.'

'As far as I can see there will not be very much. Anyone soaked in the books will have done by far the greater part of the reading to be got through. But has he enough spare time?'

'He seems to have no dissipations. He would be as happy writing the life of T. T. Waring as writing his regimental history.'

'I'll tell you what,' said Hugh; 'you sound your friend. If he is at all interested, get him in. I should like to meet him again in any case. Talking it over can't do any harm.'

Hugh's easy accord showed how desperate he must be feeling about the book's prospects. But there was still Bernard to be tackled. Hudson was unlikely to appeal to Bernard in his present mood.

'And then there is something else. Have you ever met a girl called Roberta Payne?'

Hugh shook his head and grinned uncomfortably. He always gave the impression that he considered any woman he had not himself met must live in a life of doubtful virtue.

'She is a friend of mine. I saw her the other day and she told me she had met T. T. Waring in France.'

Hugh showed interest.

'Then you actually know someone who has spoken to T. T.,' he said. 'That is nearer than I've ever got.'

'More than that. She was engaged to him.'

'What?'

'So she tells me.'

'What sort of a girl is she?'

Hugh sounded quite jealous.

'A journalist.'

'But is she pretty?'

'Not bad.'

Hugh looked doubtful. It was his omnipresent fear that some woman might be foisted on him who would turn out to be an adventuress and would blackmail him. This preoccupation made it almost impossible for him to engage a secretary. He said:

'We ought to be able to make use of this.'

'That's what I thought. She is anxious to help. Naturally, she would want a *quid pro quo.*'

'What sort of a one?' Hugh said, as if he thought that the onus was being shifted to him.

'According to what she produced, I suppose, we could pay her a sum down or give her a minute royalty.'

'I should favour money down,' said Hugh. 'Decidedly.'

'I expect Roberta would too. She said she would look in here one day soon.'

'Very well. I suppose I must see her.'

'I think you will find her sensible.'

'Oh, good,' said Hugh, but without enthusiasm. 'By the way, here is that American novel I told you about. Let me know what you think of it.'

'Anything special?'

'I don't feel happy about the chapter where Irving and Wayne listen to the whip-poor-will.'

'I'll study it.'

I took *Lot's Hometown* and went back to my room to ring up Hudson. We had spent a number of evenings together since we had first met. Sometimes Hudson would scarcely speak all the time we were together. On other occasions he would tell long stories about his childhood or describe the lines on which he thought the Army should be reorganised. When I got through to him at the Terri-torial headquarters he sounded in a good temper. I

suggested that we should dine together. He was free that
night as it happened. We arranged to meet.

Towards the end of the meal, which we ate in a
restaurant in the Strand where the diners sat shut off from
each other by high wooden stalls, I told Hudson more or
less how matters stood. He seemed quite dazed by the
suggestion that he should write the life of T. T. Waring.
At first he was too modest to admit that he had the
necessary qualifications for the job.

'Hang it all,' he said, 'I never had a line in print, you
know.'

The question of his spare time being monopolised by
such a task appeared not to worry him at all.

'Why, you know there is nothing in the world I would
like better,' he said. 'But your chief will never agree to
it, will he?'

'It is worth trying if you are prepared to take it on.'

Hudson sat for a time thinking. Then he said:

'Tell me more about the Judkins family. Do they come
from Essex?'

'I have an idea they do.'

'They are both bachelors, aren't they?'

'They are.'

'And is one of them called Paul?'

'That was the brother who died. They are called Hugh
and Bernard.'

'So one of them died? That explains things. In that
case, I believe they have a niece who married a cousin of
mine in the Burma Police.'

This was a great piece of news. Bernard was proud of
his family. It was one of the traditions of the firm, dating
from the time of Eli Judkins, that the clan should be
considered important. Hugh had always disregarded this

tradition. He proclaimed openly that he detested his relations. Few of his brother's characteristics annoyed Bernard more than this one. If Hudson could be presented as a ramification of the house of Judkins it was three-quarters of the way to persuading Bernard to commission him to write the life of T. T. Waring. I told Hudson this.

'But do you really think I carry the guns?' he said.

'Why not?'

'Oh well—of course you've told me that you yourself aren't so keen on what T. T. Waring wrote, but—well, it means a good deal to me for some reason.'

'It does to lots of people. That is why you ought to write it.'

'I shouldn't like to think that I was not going to do him justice.'

'You'll do him justice all right.'

So it was decided that Hudson should come and see Hugh the following day. He seemed too excited with the idea to want to discuss it further. I did not mention Roberta's angle on the story. There would be time for that when the contract was signed with Hudson. After dinner we went to a news film.

When we had seen the reel through, Hudson suggested that we should look in at his club. As we crossed St. James's Square he said:

'I never use the place. This is an opportunity to get some of my money's worth. Do you do this sort of thing every night?'

'More or less. Sometimes I read.'

'Or take a girl out.'

'Occasionally.'

Hudson often gave an impression that he wanted to talk about women. He always veered off the subject at the last moment. Perhaps he thought that it was a topic unsuited

84

to a man who was engaged to be married. He once began a long story about a girl he had known who sat in a tobacconist's kiosk, but I was never able to establish with any certainty precisely what had happened between them.

'I suppose you are usually working in the evening?'

'Worse luck. Though it gives you something to do.'

'You'll have plenty to do if you take on T. T. Waring.'

'We'll never be able to bring that off.'

'Don't be so sure.'

He led the way up the steps of the club. We hung up our hats and went along a passage to the smoking-room. Here several groups and single figures were bivouacked, silent or conversing in whispers, as if preparing for a sudden sortie. Passing between these and other drowsy shapes we went on into an inner room, empty except for a couple in the corner sitting with their backs to us. Here we found a sofa. Hudson ordered drinks. He said:

'Where do you go for your leave?'

'Different places. If possible abroad.'

'Do you know France well?'

'I've often been there. I wouldn't go so far as to say that I know the country well.'

'I went to Paris my first leave after I joined the regiment,' Hudson said. 'You know, I didn't enjoy myself nearly so much as I expected to.'

'Did you go alone?'

'There were three of us. It was the hell of a frost. Still, I want to try France again one day.'

'You should.'

'Of course one needs to know the language.'

The two men in the corner stood up. The taller of them, who had a black moustache and was as lean and yellow as an Asiatic, knocked out his pipe on an ash-tray. The other, short, thick, and dressed in a tweed suit and bright brown buckskin shoes, conveyed an air of tremendous spruceness. He leant with one arm on the table in front of him and struck a match. As he straightened himself and took the cigarette from his mouth his voice came across the room:

'Not tonight, Josephine. Decidedly not tonight.'

The tall man laughed. They came past us. It was only then that I saw that the shorter of the two was Eustace Bromwich. He looked very well and was evidently at the top of his form.

'Hullo, Eustace. I thought you were in France.'

'Why, hullo,' said Eustace. 'I had to come over for a day or two. That great-aunt of mine has not been feeling too good again. However, as soon as I arrived she cheered up at once. When I left her she was talking of going racing.'

'Why didn't you ring me up?'

'I had to see my lawyer and quite a lot of people who were yammering to be paid money. I haven't had a moment.'

'Let's meet.'

'I go back tomorrow.'

'What time?'

'Early in the morning. But I'll give you my address.'

'Look here, Eustace,' said the tall man, 'I must go or I shall miss the Aldershot train. I don't want to be cashiered.'

'Good-bye, old boy, and thanks for dinner,' Eustace said. 'Don't take any wooden nickels.—I say, do you mind if I sit with you for a minute or two? I'm not a member here.'

He said the last part of this to Hudson, who had been looking him up and down without much warmth, pausing for a second at the Guards tie.

'Captain Bromwich—Captain Hudson.'

'Have a drink,' said Hudson.

'That's uncommonly kind of you,' said Eustace. 'Do you

know, I believe I will. How is everyone keeping without me? I've hardly seen a soul, I have been so busy.'

'The Manasses gave a party the other day.'

'Fun?'

'Not bad. I saw Roberta there.'

'I suppose she was the only girl in the world and you were the only *goy*?'

'Absolutely the only one.'

'I'm living at Toulon now,' Eustace said. 'As a matter of fact, I saw Roberta at that wedding we last met at. She recommended the place to me. I keep a room at one of the pubs. Though sometimes I stay at other places along the coast.'

I was reminded of the story of Roberta's engagement to T. T. Waring.

'You've never met someone called Robinson who lives there?'

'Now how the hell did you come across him?' Eustace said. 'What is the low-down? He's a funny sort of beggar. I ran across him soon after I arrived there. I haven't seen him lately. He borrowed a couple of hundred francs off me, as a matter of fact, so I wouldn't mind buttonholing him again.'

'I don't know him. I heard he was engaged to someone and hoped to hear more about him from you.'

'Engaged, was he?' said Eustace. 'He didn't look the marrying sort to me. But you never know.'

'How did you happen on him?'

'I was messing about with my boat one day. He came up to me and said: "You're English, aren't you?" Well, I thought that was a piece of thundering cheek. I told him I was the Grand Duke Anton of Russia. He believed it for weeks, until one day I got sick of talking broken English to him and told him not to be such a damned fool.'

'Where did he live?'

'He had a flat on the Port. An awful hole, with never a drop of drink in the place. What on earth Robinson did with himself all day long or what he lived on I can't imagine. He once said that he earned his bread by translating, but I suspect he was a remittance man'—Eustace's voice deepened, giving warning that he was taking the shape of one of his avatars—'I shouldn't wonder if Master Robinson hadn't done something pretty beastly back in the Old Country.'

'So what happened?'

'Do you remember my telling you that an old American trout wanted to marry me?'

'The one who lent you the Rolls?'

'That was the lady. I drove it over a cliff for her, as a matter of fact. What did she do but turn up in Toulon?'

'To try and sue you for damages?'

'Not a bit of it. She'd forgotten all about the car. She just wanted me. She had the impudence to accost me there in the street. As it happened, I was on my way to Robinson's flat to try and get my two hundred francs back. I thought I would teach them both a lesson by taking her with me. Were they embarrassed? Not a bit. You might have thought the old girl was just what Robinson was waiting for. When I left them he was sitting on the ground handing her cups of tea. That was the last I saw of him.'

'Didn't you get your two hundred francs back?'

'I went along there a few days later. The flat was locked up. It has been ever since. I asked the concierge about it. She said the rent was paid up till the end of the quarter and that was all she knew about him. He was a funny devil, Robinson. Boats didn't interest him a bit.'

All this time Hudson had been sitting in silence. At first he looked as if he resented Eustace's presence. When

88

Eustace began to talk he seemed more reconciled to him. He even laughed once or twice, which was always rare with him. It was in Hudson's interests to listen, whether he liked it or not, because he might need Eustace's reminiscences of T. T. Waring almost as much as Roberta's. He could be told at a later date why he had been made to hear all this about Robinson. Eustace must have noticed that Hudson was looking out of the conversation. He turned to him and said:

'Are you keen on sailing?'

'I've never done any.'

'It's not a bad sport,' Eustace said. 'I only know two better, and one of them's drinking.'

'I might come and see you in the summer if I'm not made to sail,' I said.

'But I thought that was fixed, anyway.'

We talked for a time. Then Hudson glanced at his watch. The party broke up soon after this. Eustace scribbled his address on a sheet of club notepaper and gave it to me. I told him I would write to him later if I found that I could come out to France. We all left the club together. Hudson went off in the direction of the Horse Guards and Victoria. Eustace was staying in Jermyn Street. I walked with him as far as the corner.

'Who was that?' he said, when Hudson had left us.

I told him.

'He is probably going to write a book for Judkins & Judkins.'

'What about?'

'A life of T. T. Waring.'

'That blighter? We shan't hear any more of him now. Of all the rot I've ever read that fellow wrote the worst.'

'Did you hear anything about his death? It was near Marseilles.'

89

'I read about it in the papers.'

'You didn't know anyone who knew him?'

'I had no idea he ever went to France. I thought he was supposed to spend all his time in the desert and places like that. Well, this is where we part, old boy. Don't forget—the Hôtel de la Mer et des Amiraux.'

Hudson's appointment with Hugh was for half-past three. At about a quarter-past Hugh came up to my room with some stuff that had to be read in a hurry.

'You'd better leave *Lot's Hometown* for the moment,' he said. 'Read as much of these as you can between now and tomorrow morning and let me know what you think about the author. He used to sell well before the War. It is a question of buying up cheap rights.'

He put down on the table the pile of books he was carrying. I was looking through them when there was a knock on the door.

'Come in.'

I thought it would turn out to be Hudson arrived early. It was not. Roberta stood on the threshold. She was dressed in black with white frills. She looked unusually demure.

'I remembered where your room was,' she said, 'and came straight up. I hope I am not disturbing you.'

She turned in Hugh's direction and fixed him with those large eyes, lowering the lids a little, and looking down. Hugh went scarlet. I saw at once that he supposed she was a tart who had come to blackmail one of us, perhaps both. Roberta was between him and the door. He was trapped. The only thing to do was to explain as soon as possible who she was. Such an introduction might prejudice Hugh against her, but there was no other course to follow.

'This is Mr. Hugh Judkins, Roberta. Miss Payne has

come to tell us about her friendship with T. T. Waring.'

Hugh still looked nervous. He shook hands and suggested that all three of us should go down to his room. The stairs took a lot of negotiating because Roberta asked Hugh to lead the way. When we arrived there she began on Hugh without further delay. It was an onslaught that might have broken up someone more used than Hugh to Roberta's methods.

'Mr. Judkins, I've always wanted to meet you so much. You know, I've heard a tremendous amount about you from someone called Arthur Lipfield. He is a great admirer of yours.'

Again Hugh blushed hotly. Roberta's spy-system was remarkable. It was impossible to guess how she had discovered that Hugh knew Lipfield. By mentioning this she established an instantaneous and double hold on Hugh, because she could flatter him and at the same time quell him by her knowledge of what in the office amounted almost to a guilty secret.

'You know, I am very interested in *that* too,' said Roberta.

'Oh, yes, indeed?'

Hugh gave several little intakes of breath like a Jap. He was having a bad time. Roberta said:

'And was it really the case that something about T. T. came through? Arthur Lipfield said that you were there when it happened.'

'Well,' said Hugh, 'it was curious——'

'*Do* tell me, Mr. Judkins.'

The sooner Roberta had him to herself the better things would go. Disregarding an appealing look from Hugh, I made some excuse and left them together.

Out in the passage a creaking noise sounded on the landing below. The creaking was accompanied by heavy breathing like that of a large animal. This turned out to b

Bernard coming up the stairs. He had the appearance of having made a hearty lunch. If that was the case it had put him in a good temper. He said:

'A lovely afternoon. We ought all to be in the country.'

I expressed respectful agreement.

'Come in here,' said Bernard. 'The illustrations to *Fierce Midnights* arrived just before luncheon. I want you to go through them. Mrs. Gulliver-Lawson wrote to ask that special care should be taken about her blocks this time. She was disappointed with the last lot.'

Bernard sat down at his desk. Still breathing heavily he began to undo the parcel. While I was sorting out the proofs on a side table the house telephone buzzed. Bernard took it up.

'Hullo?' he said; and then: 'There is a Captain Hudson to see you. Shall I tell them to send him up to your room?'

'Please. I'll take these away with me, then?'

'Do,' said Bernard, who in spite of his apathy was an inquisitive man. 'Who is Captain Hudson?'

'Curiously enough, I believe he is a relation of yours.'

Bernard raised his bushy eyebrows, easing his neck in the steely grip of his collar. He said nothing.

'He spoke of having a cousin called Myrtle.'

'Certainly we have a niece called Myrtle. She married a young fellow who is in the Indian Army, I think.'

'That's the one.'

'So he's a cousin of hers, is he?'

'A cousin of her husband's.'

'What about Captain Hudson? Has he got a manuscript?'

'He came in to have a talk about something he thought he might write about.'

'What?'

'It is really hardly worth bothering you with.'

'But what is it?'

'He is a great admirer of T. T. Waring. He got it into his head that he would like to write a book about him. He has been told it would be quite impossible. But he is still keen on the idea.'

'Why should it be impossible?' Bernard said rather crossly. 'I thought a man to write a book about T. T. Waring was just what we were looking for.'

'But there are so many other candidates.'

'Nonsense.'

I was silent.

'As a matter of fact,' Bernard said, 'there is a certain amount of difference of opinion. First of all I thought Minhinnick would be the man. On consideration I am not so sure. We cannot afford to let a good man slip through our fingers.'

'I will hold out some encouragement to him, then?'

'Look here,' said Bernard, 'does Hugh know he is a relation of ours?'

'No.'

'Then why not let me see the man? If he is a connection I should like to have a word about family matters. We keep together, you know. Families have to these days if they want to survive.'

I took the illustrations and went up to my room. Hudson was standing there wearing a bowler hat. He was practising golf-strokes with his rolled umbrella.

'A wonderful thing has happened. I told Bernard Judkins you were a relation of his. He wants to interview you himself. The matter is in your hands. It is up to you to get a contract out of him.'

'But I've never set eyes on the man,' Hudson said. 'How can I——'

'Keep your head. Let him do the talking.'

'But what shall I say?'

'It doesn't matter.'

'But——'

We went downstairs and I introduced him to Bernard, and left him there. As I passed Hugh's door the sound of laughter came from the further side.

Hugh's idea was that he should give a dinner-party at which Hudson and Roberta should meet straight away.

'Miss Payne is a sensible young woman,' he said, 'and surely very good-looking. I saw at once that she would be useful to us. She is coming to dinner on Thursday to meet Hudson. I hope you will join the party.'

By the time Bernard had decided that Hudson was his own discovery and had brought him into Hugh's room as the man to write the T. T. Waring biography Roberta had left. Hugh had not taken long to arrange matters.

'He discussed T. T. Waring's books for about ten minutes,' Hudson told me later, 'and at the end of that he said he would draft a contract and send it to me as soon as possible.'

'What did Bernard do while this was going on?'

'He seemed surprised that his brother swallowed me so easily,' Hudson said. 'He just made one or two remarks about the importance of keeping the book the right length. Then he went back to his room.'

Hugh gave a similar account of the proceedings. He was pleased with himself about the dispatch with which the matters had been arranged. I thanked him for his invitation to dinner, which I accepted.

'Do you think Hudson will do?'

'I see no reason why he should not be very satisfactory,'

Hugh said. 'It is curious that he and I should have met as we did. In matters of this sort I always seem to find the right person sooner or later.'

'I wonder how he will like Roberta?'

'He is bound to like her. Nobody could help liking her, could they? And what a wonderful story that is of hers. The rescue and so on. It shows that T. T. was every bit as remarkable as one would gather from his books.'

This sounded as if Roberta had treated Hugh to a doctored version of her first encounter with T. T. Waring.

'Did you tell Hudson why he had got to meet her?'

'I only hinted at it. Perhaps as you know them both you could prepare them before the day arrives.'

Hugh was rushing things. Hudson held strong views on the subject of cosmetics, painted finger-nails, and equivocal conversation in women. He would not show his prejudices in an offensive way, but it was possible that Hugh was too optimistic. A barrier might be set up between Roberta and Hudson at this early meeting which would make their literary relations difficult.

'How old did you say Miss Payne was?'

'Twenty-five, I think.'

'She must be younger than twenty-five,' Hugh said. 'She is scarcely more than a schoolgirl. Though she has all the intelligence and charm of a mature woman. One must admit that.'

The fourth guest at Hugh's dinner-party was Miss M'Kechnie. Whether Hugh invited her because she had been the interpreter of Mimi's announcement of T. T. Waring's death; because she was the only woman of his acquaintance who was available that evening; or because in a spirit of roguishness he thought he would like to watch the effect of Roberta's impact on her, could only be guessed at. If it was the last of these, he had a good entertainment. Miss M'Kechnie took an instant dislike to Roberta which she did not attempt to conceal.

'It was wonderful of Mimi to forewarn us in that way,' she said. 'You know, I couldn't sleep all night for thinking about T. T. Waring. And then the news came in the morning.'

'The news came that night, as a matter of fact,' Hugh said.

No doubt he would have enjoyed a good set-to with Miss M'Kechnie as to whether the prophecy had emanated from the world of spirits or had been read by the medium in the six-thirty edition of the evening paper. The presence of Roberta restrained him from this. He said:

'Miss Payne knew T. T. Waring very well indeed.'

'Did you really?' said Miss M'Kechnie, without warmth.

'And Captain Hudson is going to write T. T. Waring's biography.'

'Indeed,' said Miss M'Kechnie. 'I hope he will do it well. T. T. Waring is one of my favourite authors.'

She looked round the room and sniffed. Hudson laughed and said he would do his best to write the book to her satisfaction. He said to Roberta:

'We've got to meet some time and begin our series of conversations.'

'Don't let's discuss all that now,' Roberta said. 'I'll give you my number and we can arrange a time. It is such a bore for the others to make all our plans here.'

'Right you are.'

Hudson talked more during dinner than was usual with him; and Roberta less. Hugh addressed all his remarks to Roberta and continually filled up her glass, so that if she had not carried her wine pretty well she would have been under the table by the end of the meal. Miss M'Kechnie watched them sourly. To say that she was jealous of Roberta's success with Hugh would have been perhaps hardly just to her; but at the same time she regarded Hugh as in a specialised way her own property to bicker with, and she seemed to resent his polemical attitude being vitiated by Roberta's presence.

'I hear that Mrs. Cromwell has had a lot of trouble with that young medium,' she said.

'The one who was there the night I came?' Hudson asked.

'What, again?' said Hugh, breaking into the conversation. 'That woman really is incorrigible. The young man was all right at the beginning. I suppose she flattered him and pampered him and told him he was the most wonderful medium there had ever been, until he did not know whether he was on his head or his heels. Mrs. Cromwell would corrupt a saint.'

Miss M'Kechnie laughed.

'Ridiculous, isn't it?' she said. 'At her age.'

She stared hard at Hugh when she said this.

'I never liked him, as a matter of fact,' Hugh said. 'I am not at all surprised that something of this sort has happened.'

Miss M'Kechnie said:

'That boy was as straight as a die. Anything that took place can be laid at Mrs. Cromwell's door.'

'I'm not so sure,' said Hugh.

'Perhaps you don't know so much about Mrs. Cromwell as I do.'

'I know something that Lipfield told me,' said Hugh.

He sniggered. The wrangle went on in different forms for the rest of the evening. Miss M'Kechnie rose at about a quarter to eleven and said she must go. Rather unexpectedly Roberta accepted her offer of a lift. Roberta gave the impression that she had not much taken to Hudson. It would be awkward if she refused to co-operate. Hudson and I stayed on talking to Hugh, who in the excitement of his battle of words with Miss M'Kechnie had forgotten all about T. T. Waring. It was nearly midnight when we left the flat. We walked towards Baker Street.

'What did you think of Roberta?'

'Rather nice. A bit stuck-up, I should think. Were they engaged for long?'

'Quite a short time, I think.'

In view of what she must have told Hugh there was no knowing what sort of a story Roberta would produce for Hudson.

'Was she engaged to that guardee you talked to at my club?'

'Eustace? I shouldn't imagine so. They ran round together for a time. I first met him at her flat.'

'Hugh Judkins is a queer sort of fellow,' Hudson said. 'I can't quite make him out.'

'He is not so bad really.'

'Well, I don't expect I shall be visible for some time now,' Hudson said. 'I shall set to work at once and rough out a synopsis.'

'It will be an awful sweat with your other work, I'm afraid.'

'I like work,' Hudson said. 'And look here, thanks awfully for getting all this fixed up for me. I never thought we should manage it.'

'The book is not out yet.'

'No,' he said, 'that's very true. By the way, I forgot to tell you. Beryl and I are going to get married in September after I come back from camp. I suppose we shall be having a bit of a honeymoon somewhere. That may hold up work on the book for a time.'

'That sounds all right. I shouldn't worry.'

'It's satisfactory to know that things are settled at last,' he said, 'after all this hanging about.'

5

THE cold wet summer dragged on. Deciding to overdraw at the bank, I wrote to Eustace and told him to expect me at Toulon towards the end of August. Foreign travel was a necessity. A coloured postcard of the *Monument aux Morts* arrived in due course, on the back of which in a straggling hand was written: *It's a date. Va bene. B. Mussolini.*

Hudson had not appeared for weeks. He spent all his spare time making notes on the T. T. Waring books. This engaged all his free evenings. He would not even come out to dinner. Looking back on it, I could never remember at what stage we had begun to meet often; but now that I no longer saw him regularly I realised that his affairs, bounded by the Pimleys, T. T. Waring, Lipfield's séance, and his Territorials, had become in a way part of my life, especially Hudson's stories of Lipfield as an infantry officer. But it was a private sphere shut off from the rest of existence, because Hudson rarely showed any wish to meet new people. Whether this was the outcome of shyness or a simple lack of interest it was hard to say. Now that he had retired into his shell, time passed and I forgot about the whole business. There were other matters, as it happened—of a personal sort—to occupy my attention. Besides, *Stendhal: and Some Thoughts on Violence* was long overdue. The example of Hudson's industry caused me to return to it and grind out another twenty pages.

Then one day I was returning from lunch in one of

those underground haunts in the City where financiers eat indigestible meals. I had been entertained there by a chartered accountant who wanted some belles-lettres he had written published at his own expense. On the way back to the office I ran into Lipfield coming along Old Broad Street. He was full of conversation.

'When are you going to join our little circle again?' he said. 'I hope you don't disapprove of our research work?'

'I'd like to come very much if I'm invited.'

'I believe you know the young lady Mr. Judkins always brings with him now,' said Lipfield. 'Miss Payne.'

'Miss Payne?'

The name conveyed nothing in connection with Hugh.

'Miss Roberta Payne,' Lipfield said. 'My firm has the honour and pleasure of doing a little business for her now and then. Just small investments. But she knows her own mind. I always say there is nothing like a lady when she has an instinct for the Market.'

'Oh yes. Of course. I know her well. I'd forgotten she was interested in psychical research.'

'Mr. Judkins introduced her to it. She is keen now. Very keen.'

'Is she?'

'It is encouraging,' said Lipfield, 'when a really quite beautiful young lady like that takes an interest in such matters. It contradicts all you read in the papers about the Younger Generation.'

'I agree.'

'You must come again yourself soon,' said Lipfield. 'Let me have your address. I will notify you when we have something interesting.'

'Do you still meet at Mrs. Cromwell's?'

Lipfield shook his head.

'Mrs. Cromwell is away at the moment,' he said. 'Between

you and me, there was a lot of trouble about that young medium you met there. It seems he got quite a lot of money out of her. Behaved very badly. Of course there were faults on both sides. But he oughtn't to have acted as he did. She has gone abroad for a long rest-cure. But I expect it won't be many months before we hear from her again. She is very keen.'

'She is pretty well off, I suppose?'

'Comfortable,' Lipfield said. 'I look after some of her interests. We have a Dutch medium at the moment. A lady. But——'

Lipfield pursed his lips in the direction of his nose and thrust forward his head.

'No *bonne*,' he said.

'How is your adjutant behaving? Has he been attending any more sittings?'

'Captain Hudson?' Lipfield roared with laughter. 'No, he did not seem to get on with them somehow. I say it was Miss M'Kechnie. She's a caution, that lady.'

Lipfield went into paroxysms of laughter again at the thought of Hudson and Miss M'Kechnie. Then, recovering himself, he said:

'But he's a fine fellow is Captain Hudson. And a very fine officer too. He knows about discipline. My word! But it's what you want. No good trying to be a soldier without it.'

'He keeps you all up to the mark, does he?'

'I should just about say he does,' said Lipfield. 'But I mustn't delay you any longer. I expect you are just as busy as I am myself.'

He jogged off towards Lothbury, clutching his umbrella and shrinking his shoulders as if to avoid a pursuing cohort of lamenting spirits summoned unwilling from the abyss.

On the way back to the office I reflected on what Lipfield

had said. To bring Roberta to a séance was a novel idea. For a shy man it would supply a short cut to holding her hand in the dark for a considerable period of time. I dismissed this unworthy suspicion. Roberta was an intelligent girl and a journalist. She had probably asked Hugh to take her there because she wanted to write an article on the subject. Besides, Hugh was not much interested in the frivolous side of life. He had more than once said that people exaggerated its importance when they wrote novels. He was wrapped up in his work. All the same, he had been in exceptionally high spirits for some weeks.

Back in my room, I settled down to *Lot's Hometown*. Considerable excisions had been made already; but it had returned from Bernard with orders for further expurgation. This was the third time through. My interest in the story was waning.

Late in the afternoon the telephone-bell rang.

'Hullo?'

'This is Beryl Pimley.'

'Are you in London?'

'Yes, of course.'

She sounded pleased about something.

'The family have taken a flat in Chelsea,' she said. 'We are giving a small party tomorrow. Will you come? About six o'clock.'

Before I could answer she went on:

'It is really to celebrate the announcement of our engagement. Tiger and I are going to get married in September. It will be in the paper tomorrow.'

I made the conventional remarks on this news and said that I should look forward to the party. Beryl told me the address and how to get there. She rang off. A few minutes later the bell sounded again. This time it was Hudson. We had not spoken for weeks. He was gruff.

'Congratulations.'

'What on?'

'I hear the date is fixed for your wedding.'

'Oh yes,' he said. 'That. Thanks awfully. Of course it was all decided already. It is only the announcement that is being celebrated. Look here, shall I see you at the party?'

'Yes.'

'Because there are some things I want to discuss. I was going to get in touch with you, anyway.'

'How is the book going?'

'Pretty well. That's what I want to see you about.'

He hung up the receiver. It was one of his brusque days, aggravated no doubt by nerves at the prospect of marriage.

When I left the office that evening Hugh was already on his way down the stairs. Outside in the street a warm wind was blowing. We walked together across the square. I told him that I had seen Lipfield that afternoon in the City.

'Oh yes,' Hugh said. 'I've been to several sittings recently. I took Roberta Payne to one of them, as a matter of fact—as she expressed interest. By the way, have you heard at all how Hudson is finding the Waring life?'

'I'm seeing him tomorrow. He wants to talk over some points. Did Roberta mention how their collaboration was going?'

'I think she has been very useful,' Hugh said. 'They meet at stated intervals, it seems.'

We walked on in silence for a time. Then Hugh said:

'With regard to Roberta Payne's contribution, I thought the simplest thing would be for her to have a royalty of five per cent.'

'Five per cent? Hudson himself is only getting ten, isn't he?'

'Yes, and quite enough too,' Hugh said. 'After all, he

has never written a book before. He is very lucky to have been commissioned at all. He is quite agreeable to that distribution of a fifteen per cent. royalty, which I suppose we should have had to pay if we had employed a professional author. Really, I don't think he would have been able to write the book at all if Roberta Payne had withheld her information.'

'She has produced a lot, has she?'

'It was a remarkable thing that meeting of hers with T. T. It has its moving side.'

'It certainly has.'

One day I hoped to find out what sort of a story Roberta had told Hugh, that differed so much from the version she had considered suitable for myself.

'She is a very useful find, that young woman,' Hugh said. 'She has promised to send me some articles of hers that have appeared in various papers, with a view to reproducing them in book form. I thought it might be decorated by that artist friend of Shirley Handsworth's—I can never remember his name—and done at six shillings. Or possibly five.'

Hugh knew as well as I did that a book of Roberta's collected newspaper articles would not sell a dozen copies. He was trifling with her girlish optimism if he had held out any hope that they would appear under the Judkins & Judkins imprint. Alternatively, he had already decided that he would publish them because he was in the palm of Roberta's hand.

'What does Shirley Handsworth think about not getting the job to do himself?'

Hugh coughed and frowned.

'I am looking about for something else, to prevent him from being disappointed,' he said. 'We don't want disappointed authors. Of course he would never have done, really. I was rather surprised that you were keen about it. Besides, Bernard was against him. One has to consider Bernard's opinions even when they sometimes differ radically from one's own. After all, he is my elder brother.'

'And I suppose he will settle Minhinnick?'

'Minhinnick was never a serious danger,' Hugh said, chuckling, 'even from the start. But I hope I have found the right man now. I think somehow I have.'

The Pimleys had established themselves in a small, dark, red-brick block of flats in a side street off the Embankment, not far from Battersea Bridge. Beryl had insisted on being married in London, in the face of some opposition from her parents on account of the additional expense. A relation of Mrs. Pimley with a house in Oxford Square had offered to lend it for the reception, so in the end Beryl had her way. Winefred, on the other hand, had wanted to stay by herself in the country, coming up only on the day of the wedding. She was not allowed to do this, as the Pimleys thought it would be a good thing for her to enjoy the tail-end of the season in London. When everything was arranged the grandfather gave out that he too wished to come to London with the family. Efforts were made to dissuade him. These were unsuccessful. Captain Pimley gave as his reason that it was his last chance of seeing Piccadilly again. Although the probability of his getting so far east as Hyde Park Corner was remote, he met every argument by repeating this. That was why he was now sitting in the corner of the drawing-room, half facing the wall, with his tartan rug wrapped round his knees. These details were supplied by Hudson.

The other guests consisted of two cousins of the Pimleys, large bony girls who worked in some charity organisation;

one of Hudson's Territorials; and two middle-aged men in black coats and striped trousers whose names were not revealed but who behaved as if they were relations. Captain Pimley seemed to be enjoying himself. He was nodding his head and sometimes beating time with his finger, as one who hears distant music. Winefred stood near the piano, an upright one, watching the room as if she hoped that the earth would open and engulf it.

'So that is why they are all here,' said Hudson, coming to the end of his account of the Pimley family's movements, 'and while they stay I am expected to amuse them.'

'What steps are you taking to do so?'

'That was one of the things I wanted to ask you about. My Territorials are giving a subscription dance in their drill-hall. I'll explain all the details about it later, if you are interested. The point is, can you help me out by joining my party for it?'

'When is it?'

'Today fortnight.'

'I think I can come.'

'I can't pretend it will be very amusing,' Hudson said. 'In fact, so far as you are concerned the only bright spot will be the spectacle of Lipfield in mess kit.'

'And you are taking a party?'

'I am taking Beryl and Winefred. Between you and me, I am fed up at having to go to the damned show at all. But it's unavoidable.'

'Why not take Beryl alone?'

'I've let myself in for taking the whole lot of them now. It's too late to get out of it.'

'Including the grandfather?'

'Oddly enough, no. The General won't come either. It would be doing me an awfully good turn if you could join us.'

'I'll come.'

'You realise you will go as Winefred's partner?'

'I'll make my will. How is the book getting on?'

Hudson, who had been drumming on the wall with his knuckles, stopped suddenly.

'That was the other business I wanted to talk to you about,' he said. 'I've discovered a rather curious thing.'

'About T. T. Waring's private life?'

'In that direction I've made absolutely no headway. Where he came from I can't imagine. I've tried all the Waring families in the telephone-book and lots of others. None of them seem to know anything about him. I can't even find out what his initials stood for. This is in regard to his books rather than him.'

'He always liked it to be hinted that Waring wasn't his real name.'

'I don't think it can have been.'

'You've heard all Roberta has got to say by this time?'

'Yes.'

'What do you make of that?'

'It doesn't throw much light on the situation. After all, it is quite in keeping with the rest of his behaviour that he should cloak his identity under the name of Robinson.'

'But what about the engagement?'

'My explanation of that,' said Hudson, speaking very slowly, 'is that he was carried away on impulse. After all, I suppose Roberta Payne is one of the most beautiful and attractive women one could possibly meet.'

He said these words in a tone that surprised me. His manner often became unexpectedly serious. He spoke now with such exaggerated conviction that for a moment it sounded like irony.

'In the creed of an artist like T. T. Waring,' he went on in the same tone, 'women had no place. But when he met

Roberta Payne his self-mastery left him for a space. He became as other men. Then he saw that such things were not for him. Before any irreparable damage was done he went on his way.'

'Perhaps that was it.'

After all, Hudson had to compose the book out of the material at hand. There was no point in his publishers' representative making tendentious criticisms of the subject. No doubt it was easier to write about someone thought of always in these heroic terms. Perhaps that was how Stendhal should be tackled. It was interesting to note the effect of soaking in the works of T. T. Waring on Hudson's conversational style.

'But what is the thing you wanted to discuss? I'm afraid I got you off your subject.'

'Are you two ever going to stop talking shop?' said Mrs. Pimley, pouring out for both of us a second dose of some brackish cocktail kept in a jug. 'Since Tiger became an author none of us ever see anything of him at all. It's too bad.'

She was distracted from us by her father-in-law, who had begun to make signs to indicate that he wanted to be moved further from the gas-fire, which was alight in spite of the comparative warmth of the day. She turned away across the room. Hudson began again.

'There were views expressed in the first book about Ceylon,' he said, 'that I wanted to compare with those of some other writers on the subject. I went to the British Museum.'

'But there were probably hundreds of books about Ceylon there. Did you get them all out?'

'Quite a lot of them. Among others, I sent for one that had been published in India in the 'seventies. I can't imagine why I picked it out.'

'Well?'

'It was in a dilapidated state with paper covers and printed in Bombay. I was glancing through it when I came across a passage that seemed familiar. I went on reading and was struck by the way the author—who was anonymous —seemed to agree with all T. T. Waring wrote about the same place. I had T. T. Waring's book with me. I compared the two passages. What do you think?'

'How should I know?'

Hudson again began to drum on the wall. He said: 'The fact is, chunks of this book were incorporated almost bodily into the T. T. Waring.'

'What was the book called?'

'Something non-committal, like *A Traveller in Ceylon* or *Memoirs of a Journey in Ceylon.*'

'So he added plagiarism to his other eccentricities?'

'Of course I don't mean to say the book was reproduced word for word. On the contrary, all the interesting parts, the thoughts on life, and so on, are all T. T.'s. And the descriptions of scenery are put into finer words and better English. But the places dealt with are the same. Some of the incidents are very similar.'

'After all, most of Stendhal's first book was copied from a work that had already appeared in Italian.'

'Oh, was it?' Hudson said. 'Well, I don't see why not, really. If the author is big enough. And to my mind T. T. is big enough. But it just raised the question of what I should say about it, having made the discovery. I don't want to give something away to the public that will make them think badly of T. T. Waring. On the other hand, it seems only honest to mention it in a book that is supposed to deal comprehensively with his life and work.'

'I should do just whichever you feel like.'

'It's sailing a bit near the wind to use a lot of another fellow's book.'

'It certainly is.'

'I shall have to think it over,' said Hudson. 'I just wanted to get your view. Meanwhile, I can rely on you to come to this ghastly hop?'

'Yes.'

'Dinner is here. At a quarter to eight.'

We were joined by General Pimley.

'I've been thinking about that stamp collection of yours,' he said, 'and it seems to me that you and I might be useful to each other. If you feel like selling it you will get a better price from me than you would if you went to a dealer, and I shall get the stamps cheaper than if I bought them in the ordinary way. Of course it is true you might get a fancy price in auction, but that is always a gamble.'

'Shall I bring the album along for you to look through?'

'That would be perfectly splendid.'

'I'll bring it on the night of the Territorial dance.'

'I'll look through it. Then we can meet again and have a good haggle.'

'Very well.'

Mrs. Pimley reappeared. She said:

'I'm so glad to hear that you can join us for the dance. Will you come over and have a word with my father-in-law? He noticed you were here and remembered meeting you in the country. He really is a wonder, isn't he?'

She led me across to where Captain Pimley was sitting. He showed no interest and appeared to have forgotten his demand during the period that had elapsed between asking to speak to me and my arrival at his side. A chair, carved in the Spanish manner, and exquisitely uncomfortable, was moved up. Mrs. Pimley left me beside the old man. At first he was silent. Then, without turning his head, he said:

'Beryl is to get . . . married.'

'Yes. Quite soon.'

'What . . .'

'Soon. Quickly. She is to be married quickly.'

Captain Pimley nodded his head. The answer seemed to please him. He said:

'Tiger is writing a . . . a . . . a . . .'

'. . . a book.'

'What is . . . it?'

'It's a life of T. T. Waring.'

'Are you . . .'

'My firm is publishing it. I think it should be very good.'

There was a long pause while Captain Pimley thought this over. Then he said quite clearly and with the emphasis he sometimes managed to put into his sentences:

'I once wrote a . . . book.'

'What was it about?'

He began to laugh again to himself, shaking his head. The rug showed signs of slipping from his knees. I lifted it back for him. He said:

'That was a long time . . . ago.'

'When?'

'A very long time . . . ago.'

Mrs. Pimley came up.

'Now you mustn't tire yourself,' she said, looking down at him. 'Don't you want to go to your room now?'

Captain Pimley muttered something. He suddenly lost all his animation. Mrs. Pimley seemed to take the mumblings as an assent, because she began to make preparations for moving him. I said good-bye, but he did not answer.

His transition was still in progress when I left the flat.

Hugh continued to show an exceptionally good humour in spite of minor anxieties at the office. The chief of these was Shirley Handsworth. Shirley had caused a lot of trouble when he found that arrangements had been made for someone else to write the life of T. T. Waring. To prevent him from offering himself to another publisher Hugh suggested that Shirley should set to work on an autobiography. Shirley was satisfied with this suggestion and the promise of an increased advance of royalties. Bernard, surprisingly, made no difficulties when Hugh showed him the contract for this work. Only at the last moment, when Hugh was leaving the room, Bernard admitted that he on his part had arranged for Minhinnick to write his autobiography as a similar recompense. Hugh grumbled a great deal; but in the circumstances he could hardly do more than this. Both authors were now at work on the stories of their respective lives. Shirley's career must have included some curious and entertaining episodes, though it was unlikely that any of these would be mentioned. Minhinnick's existence, on the other hand, had been passed in a state of dullness that rivalled that of Bernard Judkins himself. Hugh remarked that his only hope was that Minhinnick might take so long to write an account of himself and the tedious people he had met that death would intervene.

'I must say I am looking forward to my holiday,' Hugh said, discussing the matter. 'Authors are very tiring. Where are you going this year?'

'France.'

'They say those cruises up the Scandinavian coast are enjoyable,' Hugh said. 'I thought of taking one of those at the end of July or beginning of August.'

'Will it be all right if I go at the end of August?'

'Yes, yes. It doesn't matter if we overlap by a day or two. I shall be back by the first of September. Everything is quite well ahead, I think. What has happened to *Lot's Hometown*?'

'It has gone off to the printer.'

'Let's hope it will turn out to be our autumn success. I showed the spare copy of it to Roberta Payne the other day. She thought quite highly of it. I believe her opinion is of value.'

'I'm sure it is.'

'And by the way,' said Hugh, 'she gave me some of those articles she spoke of. I found them exceedingly amusing. In fact, I have put them in hand. They won't show much in the way of profit, but we can't lose much on them either. I thought I would look after the production of the book myself. We might make quite a pretty thing of it. It's good for prestige to throw off a little something like that now and then.'

'And then I suppose we shall have an option on her memoirs?'

'So you've heard about the memoirs?' said Hugh. 'She told me I was to say nothing about them. Of course they were really what I had my eye on. I think they should be very good indeed. Something really out of the way.'

He seemed a little disappointed that Roberta's memoirs should not have remained a secret between himself and her; but pleased that his foresight in making sure of this prize should be revealed.

6

THE front door of the Pimleys' flat opened before I had time to ring. General Pimley, wearing an opera-hat and black overcoat, came out. He looked like an immensely distinguished conjuror.

'On my way to dine with some cronies at the club,' he said. 'Turned out of my own house. That's what it comes to.'

He seemed in the best of tempers at the prospect of spending the evening away from his family.

'My wife is going to be rather late,' he said. 'She tore her dress while she was changing. You will find the girls in there. Mind you have a jolly time.'

'I brought my stamp-album along for you to have a look at.'

'You did? Splendid. Where is it?'

General Pimley took the album and propped it up on the window-ledge. He began to look quickly through the loose-leaved pages.

'Ah,' he said, 'some postmasters' issues. I'm interested in locals. No Confederates, I suppose? But I mustn't stay now. It's awfully good of you to have brought these. Will you leave them for me to look through?'

'Of course.'

'Give the album to my wife. She will keep it for me.'

He moved off towards the lift as if he feared that some mischance might compel him to accompany the party to the dance. I went into the hall of the flat and towards the drawing-room. Approaching the open door I heard Beryl's voice:

'If you don't like him why didn't you ask a young man of your own? Tiger gave you the chance.'

Then Winefred:

'I knew perfectly well that Tiger would insist on one of his own friends.'

They were in the middle of a row. The situation was embarrassing. If I went in at once it would be obvious that I had overheard the words that had just been spoken. There could be no doubt about the meaning of these. It seemed best to delay for a few seconds my arrival in the drawing-room, in the hope that the air would clear. I paused and straightened my white tie in the looking-glass hanging above the umbrella-stand. However, things seemed to be going from bad to worse. From irritation Beryl's voice turned to rage.

'How dare you criticise Tiger! You're not fit to black his boots. You know he puts up with all your rudeness without ever saying a word.'

The sound of Winefred's goatish laugh came. She said:

'All the same, you must admit that he likes his own way?'

'Why shouldn't he?'

'Why not indeed? All I said was that I did not specially look forward to an evening spent in the company of two men, neither of whom I care for. And you fly into a rage.'

At this moment a door opened in the passage at right angles to the wall. I was still standing in front of the mirror waiting for tempers in the drawing-room to improve. All at once in the glass was reflected the figure of Mrs. Pimley, dressed only in her underclothes and clearly in search of a maid.

'Beatrix,' she called, 'Beatrix. The tape has broken again.'

She was looking in the direction away from the hall. At any moment she might turn and see me in the same glass that presented this unconventional view of herself. In any case, I could not hang about outside indefinitely while the sisters finished their quarrel. They might continue for hours. I stepped quickly into the drawing-room. As I came through the door Beryl said:

'Why didn't you invite the young man you are always having assignations with in the garden?'

She was standing by the mantelpiece in a white evening-dress, holding a cocktail-shaker. Her faintly-sneering expression, due as much to the shape of her lips as to conscious irony of manner, had increased. Winefred's face, above the dreadful mauve garment she was wearing, had the yellowish tinge it always assumed when she was angry. Her eyes were shining with rage. Both of them were too engrossed in each other to take much notice of my arrival.

'Have a drink,' said Beryl. 'What do you think has happened? Winefred has got a young man she has been having dates with for ages and she won't tell me anything about him. She thought I didn't know.'

'I didn't think so,' Winefred said. 'I realise by this time that you ferret out everything.'

'I suppose that was why you wanted to stay in the country?'

'Naturally.'

Beryl had turned the tables on Winefred, who was now by far the angrier of the two.

'Anyway, I haven't ferreted out what he looks like,' Beryl said. 'I've only seen his back. That is why I am so curious about him. Let's hear all. What does he do, for example?'

'He is at Sandhurst.'

'A G.C.?'

'Oh no. Not by any chance. He is one of the staff-sergeants and he has a big waxed moustache.'

'Well, he might be an instructor,' Beryl said.

'I suppose you think I shouldn't have any success with a young man. I know you imagine you have a complete monopoly of sex-appeal.'

'Don't be so idiotic. Some of the instructors aren't old. Besides, you always used to say how nice Major Logwick was. He was one of the only men you have ever had a good word for.'

'He squinted.'

'Never mind. You liked him. Is your chap in the Senior Term?'

'Yes.'

'What is his name?'

'Why should I tell you?'

'Don't then.'

'I will. It's Lal.'

Now that Winefred showed herself prepared to give definite information Beryl took on a more conciliatory tone. She must have thought that she had allowed things to go too far. She said:

'What a funny name. Is it Scotch or Cornish or something? What is his Christian name?'

'I usually call him Ram.'

There was silence. Beryl started. I wondered if the suspicion that had occurred me had struck her too. It had. I could almost see it creeping like poison through her whole body.

'Winefred,' she said, 'he's not *black*?'

Winefred threw down the book she had been holding. It fell on to an occasional table on which the glasses stood, making them quiver and tingle. She almost screamed.

'I suppose *you* would call him black. You lump all races together who aren't your own anæmic colour. Indians—Africans—Maoris—everybody. Don't you realise that the Chinese were at the height of their civilisation before the Greeks and Romans were ever heard of?'

'But what have the Greeks and Romans got to do with it?' said Beryl, thoroughly upset by this disclosure. 'Oh, Winefred, you must give him up. What would people say?'

'I don't know or care. We're engaged. I suppose you thought that was something that could only happen to you?'

The scene was put an end to abruptly by the arrival of Mrs. Pimley. She came briskly into the room, full of apologies for having kept us waiting so long. Beryl was not far from tears. She turned away, agitating the cocktail-shaker. Her mother, still fussed about her own troubles, noticed nothing.

'But where is that naughty Tiger?' Mrs. Pimley said, looking round the room. 'I find I am not the last after all. I think I am ready for a cocktail, dear. Winefred, something has happened to your hair. On the left side——'

'I've brought my old stamp album here. I met General Pimley on the door-step. He asked me to give it into your charge until he had time to inspect it.'

'How frightfully interesting! Let's look at it now.'

We looked at the stamps while we waited for Hudson to turn up. Mrs. Pimley chattered away. Neither of the girls spoke much. It was some minutes before Hudson arrived. At last there was the sound of his spurs clanking in the hall. I had never before seen him in any sort of uniform. The scarlet jacket altered his appearance considerably, on the whole for the better. But he looked tired and worried.

'Doesn't Tiger look nice in mess kit?' Beryl said, taking

his arm and stroking the facings of the Royal Westmorelands.

'Doesn't he?'

Winefred watched them, grinning to herself. Hudson
disengaged his arm quite roughly. He took the drink Mrs.
Pimley held out to him.

'I'm sorry I'm late,' he said. 'Everything seemed to hold
me up this evening.'

'Let's go and have some food,' said Mrs. Pimley, as the
maid announced dinner. 'I'm quite hungry and I'm sure
all of you must be too.'

Considering what had gone before, dinner passed off
fairly well. Mrs. Pimley's mind was fixed on her torn dress.
She showed no sign of suspecting that anyone's temper
was ruffled. Hudson was gloomy and preoccupied so that
he seemed unaware of his surroundings. Both sisters must
have been ashamed of having spoken as they had in front
of a third person. Winefred began to make some conversation about books. Beryl appeared to be so horrified at the
prospect of a coloured brother-in-law that fear of this con-
tingency took the place of any bitterness she had previously
felt for her sister.

'I've borrowed a closed car to take us there,' Mrs. Pimley
said. 'You will have to sit next to the chauffeur, Tiger, and
tell him the way.'

Hudson left his grapefruit unfinished.

'I've got my own car with me,' he said, 'but I'll go on
ahead. The chauffeur can follow me.'

'How is T. T. Waring getting on?' I asked.

'Who?' said Hudson.

'Aren't you writing a book about a man called that?'

'Oh, T. T. Waring? Yes.'

Hudson laughed.

'He's getting along all right,' he said.

'Aren't you feeling well tonight, Tiger?' Beryl said.

Hudson's need to have a second guess before he remembered who T. T. Waring was must have struck her as odd.

'Perfectly well,' Hudson said.

Mrs. Pimley said:

'I sometimes wish you hadn't decided to write this book, Tiger. It's too much for you with your soldiering. I'm sure it is too much.'

'You know,' she said to me, 'you are to blame for this. Tiger is always worn out now whenever we see him.'

'It is my job to make people slave away at writing books. Messrs. Judkins & Judkins pay me for doing it.'

'It is very wicked of you,' she said. 'You ought to be ashamed of yourself.'

'Who will be there tonight, Tiger?' Beryl said.

'Wives, sisters, and sweethearts of Territorials.'

'Will there be anyone amusing?'

'I have explained before,' said Hudson, 'that it is not my place to run down the battalion of which I am the adjutant. But they are not exactly a crack regiment. If you want to know, I don't expect there will be anyone very amusing.'

'That's a pity,' Winefred said.

Hudson did not answer. Conversation died down over the cutlets. I asked how Captain Pimley was enjoying London. Mrs. Pimley said:

'He has gone to bed now, of course. He liked the party very much. I hear he had a talk with you about books. He is wonderful, isn't he?'

'Wonderful.'

Hudson and I were left together over the coffee, while the women went off to prepare for the drive. Hudson said:

'Is there anything more in that decanter?'

121

'No.'

'I thought not.'

'Shall I come in your car?'

'I'd rather be alone,' Hudson said, 'if you don't mind packing in with all of them.'

He was either extremely put out by something or deeply depressed by the thought of the evening ahead of him. I had seen him despondent before, but never so thoroughly as this.

'We're ready,' Mrs. Pimley piped.

The party went down in the lift to where an ancient Chevrolet was waiting to take us to the Territorial headquarters, which were in a remote district of South London.

The gymnasium was draped with flags and the floor surrounded by small painted gold chairs hired for the occasion. At one end of the room some silver cups rested on a table covered with green baize cloth. At the other end stood a rack holding swords and muskets, and beside this a shako under a glass dome, the accoutrements of an earlier generation of martial citizens. Several Territorials were already dancing to a band that had not yet warmed up to the pitch that might be expected of it later in the evening. Hudson introduced two or three officers. Lipfield, who was said to be bringing a party, had not yet arrived. Hudson went off with Beryl. I asked Winefred for a dance.

It seemed best to make no reference to what had gone before, not even to express the best of wishes on her engagement. There would be time for that when it was officially announced. Keeping off the subject proved too great a strain for Winefred herself.

'I suppose you are on Beryl's side,' she said as we moved round the room.

'In regard to what?'

'My engagement.'

'Really, I don't think it is any of my business.'

'You are the only person who has ever seen Ram.'

'Me?'

'Don't you remember when you stayed with us? You asked if we had an Oriental gardener.'

'So that was Ram?'

'He is so ambitious. I am sure he will do well.'

'I'm sure he will.'

'He has remarkable gifts. He tells wonderful fortunes; and he is very well read.'

'I suppose it is quite an achievement to have got to the R.M.C. at all?'

'What do you mean?'

This had been the wrong thing to say.

'Well, it not so easy. The brother of a girl I knew failed. In the end he went on the stage. He made a hit tap-dancing in Birmingham.'

'Was he an Indian?'

'Scotch.'

'I am not at all sure that Ram will go into the Army. He sometimes thinks he would do better in some other walk of life.'

'There always a place for an able man.'

Winefred did not seem altogether satisfied. She abandoned the subject of Ram and said at the top of her voice that she thought middle-aged men looked silly in short red coats and tight blue trousers. Fortunately the band stopped soon after this. We returned to the corner of the room where Mrs. Pimley was sitting. While we were talking to her the C.O. asked Beryl for the next dance. Winefred retired to the cloak-room. I went out to smoke a cigarette in the lobby, where refreshment tables had been arranged. Hudson was standing there talking to some people who had just arrived. He was doing his best to be pleasant. It looked as if he was finding it uphill work. When he saw me he said:

'I wish they would pull those blasted curtains. There's draught enough to blow everyone out of the window. Why aren't you doing your duty dancing?'

'Why aren't you? What's wrong this evening? You're biting everybody's head off.'

'Liver, I suppose.'

'Sure it isn't overwork on T. T. Waring?'

'That's the one bright spot.'

At that moment an orderly came up and said:

'Can I speak to you for a moment, sir?'

Hudson went off with him. I explored the refreshments. It was soon after this that Lipfield's party arrived.

There were eight of them. First of all Lipfield and Mrs. Lipfield, a big woman with a lot of yellow metallic hair; then a couple I did not know, clearly a husband and wife, who looked like business friends of Lipfield; after them came a girl who might have been their daughter, with a man whose face was familiar, whom I recognised later as Pemberthy, the supposed Sudan district-commissioner who had been at the séance where I had first met Hudson. But it was none of these that was the big surprise. The last pair to come into the room stole the act. They were Hugh Judkins and Roberta Payne.

There was no reason why they should not be there. It was natural for Lipfield to take a party; Hugh was a friend of Lipfield; Roberta was an acquaintance of Hugh; she was the sort of girl any man might be glad to bring to a dance if she would come. But a Territorial drill-hall was the last place in the world I expected to meet either of them.

124

I went over to talk to Hugh. I thought he would be equally surprised to see me. Instead of this his first words were:

'I don't think anyone has brought a more beautiful partner than myself.'

'Roberta?'

'Yes,' said Hugh, giggling. 'Not Mrs. Lipfield.'

He had never shown form like this before. Roberta certainly looked lovely. She kept on glancing round the room as if she were looking for somebody. There could be no doubt now about there being something on between herself and Hugh. He had a hold over her or he would never have been able to persuade her to come with him to such an entertainment. I knew her well enough for that. Unless her real life, her mysterious secret background, was set in functions of this sort. The fact that Judkins & Judkins were publishing her collected articles had no doubt something to do with her presence at the Territorial headquarters.

'Been among the spooks lately?' said Pemberthy. 'I hear from Judkins that Mimi guessed right the night you came.'

'About T. T. Waring, you mean?'

'That's the chap. Anyway, she made me get hold of some of his books by her squeakings. I'm grateful for that. I enjoyed them, I can tell you.'

Then I heard someone at my elbow say:

'Well, I'm damned!'

It was Hudson. He had come back and was standing beside me. I looked round at him. He was staring at Roberta. And then all at once the explanation of why Roberta had seemed to search round the room when she arrived was made clear. She wanted to see Hudson because he was in love with her. That was why she had allowed Hugh to bring her to the dance. Roberta saw Hudson gaping at her and waved. He went across and took her hand.

'What about a dance?' he said.

Roberta did not answer. She put her arm through his. They went off together.

'I thought you——' said Hugh.

She did not hear him. He was left grinning irritably at the place where she had been standing. Lipfield, whose appearance in mess-kit fully justified Hudson's promise of a spectacle worth any hardship, took my arm.

'I don't think you know my wife,' he said. 'You mustn't ask her about our sittings. She isn't interested. When I attend them she goes to the cinema.'

As it happened, one of the Territorials introduced me to his sister, who (though differently dressed) was strongly reminiscent of Picasso's *Femme à la chemise*. The advantages of spending the rest of the evening in her company were evident. It is unnecessary to labour the point. Winefred had said that she did not want to dance any more because she had a headache. Beryl was getting on well with the Colonel. Anyway, she was Hudson's responsibility. The thought that Hudson had fallen for Roberta went out of my head as soon as it had come into it.

Whenever I saw Hudson, whose bright-blue lapels and cuffs made him conspicuous against the white facings of the Territorial uniforms, he was dancing with Roberta. Hugh, never an expert at steering, continually collided with other couples while he partnered Mrs. Lipfield. I saw this without attaching any special significance to it. Only the day after parties events take shape in relation to each other. At the time they do not register. Mrs. Pimley was looking glum; but this was not unusual in a chaperon, especially one with a daughter like Winefred. I danced once with Roberta, who explained that she herself had asked Hugh to bring her because she had never before been anywhere of the sort. It was not until much later in the evening, when the time to go home was approaching, that unusual things began to happen.

There was a sort of yard, too small to be called a parade-ground, outside the headquarters, where some of the cars were parked round a captured German gun. It was a warm night. I was sitting out with the *Femme à la chemise,* or rather walking back to the drill-hall after a breath of fresh air. From the opposite direction Hudson came quickly, nearly running into us.

'Oh, good-night,' he said. 'I've just been saying good-bye to the Pimleys. I think they want to go home now. They are looking for you.'

'All right, good-night.'

He did not say any more and went off towards his car. Then he must have remembered that he had not answered and shouted:

'Good-night.'

We went through the door of the building into a dimly-lighted stone-paved hall. A woman was standing here trying to put on a coat. She had somehow twisted the sleeve, so that she could not get her arm into it.

'Hell!' she said, as we came towards her.

It was Roberta. I helped her into the garment.

'Just the person I wanted to see,' she said. 'Will you be an angel and tell Hugh I suddenly felt dog-tired and had a chance of a lift to my door-step? I knew it was out of Hugh's way to bring me home, so I'm taking it. Thank him a million times for the party. Or two million. I can afford it. I adored everything. Say I know it is terribly rude of me to leave like this without saying good-bye, but the people were already in the car and I had to take the chance at once.'

She ran down the steps and waved her hand. A minute later there sounded the peculiar roar Hudson's car made when he started the engine. The little Picasso looked after Roberta as if she had never before seen anything like her.

Further inside we found the Pimleys, dressed and ready to set out for home. Mrs. Pimley was fussed.

'Wherever have you been?' she said. 'We thought we should have to go home without you.'

This was evidently not the chief cause of her worry, because she went on:

'Tiger has already said good-night. I don't think he was feeling very well this evening anyway. I'm sure he overworks.'

'I'll be with you in a second. I've got to give a message to Hugh Judkins.'

'Please be quick,' she said.

I found Hugh at the bar. He was engaged in a violent argument with Pemberthy about the moral aspects of psychometry. Lipfield was close by, keeping the ring. Both Hugh and Pemberthy were quite angry by this time.

'Roberta had the offer of a lift to her door. She had to decide quickly as the car was ready to go. She took it, and asked me to thank you two million times for bringing her, and to present her apologies for not being able to say good-bye.'

'What?' said Hugh. 'Do you mean to say she has gone?'

'She said she was frightfully sorry not to see you before she went. As it was out of your way to take her home she thought it best to take the chance.'

'But——'

Hugh was angry.

'And then take the Witch of Endor,' said Pemberthy. 'What have you got to say about her?'

'It was really very silly of her,' said Hugh. 'I should like to have seen her home.'

He turned to grapple verbally with Pemberthy. I said good-night to them all and returned to the Pimleys. They had left the building. I found them already sitting in the car. Beryl had a handkerchief rolled up in her hand. She dabbed her nose from time to time and stared out of the window. Winefred, in spite of, or perhaps because of, the fact that she had only danced about three times, was holding up well.

'I hope you enjoyed yourself,' she said.

'Very much, thank you.'

The chauffeur lost his way once or twice among the road-junctions and tram-lines. The night was now sultry. Mrs. Pimley was despondent. She did not speak much except to say once:

'Tiger should take a tonic.'

Beryl sniffed for a time. Then she seemed to recover herself. No doubt she and Hudson had had differences before and she had decided that his attentions to Roberta were not to be taken too seriously. Winefred went to sleep.

We crossed back over the river. I was glad that the drive was at an end, and asked to be put down on the far side of the bridge. After thanking them for the party I took a taxi the rest of the way home.

Hugh had various interviews the following day. There was an American publisher who stayed two hours and a quarter. Later, Mrs. Gulliver-Lawson came in to inspect the revised proofs of her illustrations and took up a great deal of everyone's time. She was followed by two literary agents and a paper-maker. In fact, it was only after the week-end that there was an opportunity to take the accumulated manuscripts into Hugh's room. When I did so he was standing with his hands in his pockets, looking out of the window at the Square garden.

'Are any of those any use?'

'No.'

'Send them back, then.'

His manner had changed. All the high spirits shown during the previous weeks had gone. He seemed in the deepest dejection. It was rare for him not to want to glance through even the most unpromising collection of manuscripts.

'I get very sick of these damned manuscripts,' he said. 'Really, I sometimes wonder whether I won't go back to schoolmastering.'

This was a funny way to talk. Hugh had never said anything like that before, ever since I had known him. All his references to his earlier profession had been distinctly disparaging. He may not have wanted to become a publisher in the first place, but once he had taken it up the profession had appeared to absorb all his interests. Something must be wrong.

'After all, one was being some use doing that,' he said. 'At least I suppose one was. Do you ever think of the futility of all these books?'

'If I did it would keep me awake at night.'

'At least one was teaching someone something.'

'It was only a form of abetting the writing of more books.'

'The holidays were good.'

'Why don't you take a holiday now?'

'I can't leave till August.'

'Are you still thinking of going on that Scandinavian cruise?'

Hugh shrugged his shoulders.

'That might be enjoyable,' he said, 'if one had just the

right person to go with. I don't know that I should like it much alone.'

'Why not find someone to go with?'

Hugh looked suspicious.

'What do you mean?' he said.

It had not occurred to me that what I had said could be supposed to carry any peculiar meaning.

'There must be lots of people you know who want to go away in August. Why not ask one of them to go with you? That's all.'

Hugh thought for a moment.

'I believe you're right,' he said.

'Besides, Scandinavia is all the go now.'

'I suppose it is.' His face brightened a little.

'How did you enjoy the Territorial dance?'

This plunged him back into his earlier state of gloom. He said:

'I can't think why I went. I never liked that sort of thing. Now I am too old. Besides, Lipfield and his friends are such fearfully irksome people.'

'How did your argument with Pemberthy end?'

'It wasn't an argument. I was telling him certain established facts. Unfortunately he was too thick-headed to take them in. He has a typical bureaucrat's outlook on life.'

'It was funny our all meeting there.'

'Very funny,' said Hugh.

He began to glare out of the window again. Rain was falling gently. It looked as if he wanted to be left alone.

'There is nothing special for me to read?'

'No.'

When I returned to my room I found a letter from Hudson lying on the table. It asked me to come round and see him after dinner that evening; and not to bother to answer if I could not do so. The note had been propped up by the new office-boy on the third volume of Stendhal's *Journal.* I found my place and read a page or two of this work. In these tortuous emotions there might be consolation for Hugh. It would be worth suggesting that he should read or re-read the diaries. Hugh sometimes gave the impression that there were imponderable forces bottled up inside him. I remembered the words of the young man who had been my predecessor as a Judkins & Judkins reader and who was now working in documentary films. I had met him at a party given by some rich Left Wing people in Hampstead, to which I had accidentally allowed myself to be taken.

'Mark my words,' he had said, 'we shall see Hugh Judkins's face under the peak of a Salvation Army cap before we've finished. Or else he'll be tramping Piccadilly holding a banner stating that the Day of Judgment is at hand.'

Hudson's discovery that T. T. Waring had lifted material for his own purposes from an earlier book on Ceylon did not unduly surprise or shock me. No one who has had to 'get up' some particular subject, and to do this has read all the available books dealing with it, can have failed to notice that a good deal of plagiarism takes place, sometimes inevitably if the same ground has to be covered. But Hudson had been worried by the apparent dishonesty of doing this. I supposed that he wanted a further talk about whether or not he was to mention the matter. When he opened the door of his flat his face was lugubrious. He was taking it more seriously than I had supposed.

'Come in,' he said.

The books of military history had been replaced by the entire works of T. T. Waring and several atlases and notebooks, which now littered the table. As I sat down in the arm-chair I noticed that the photograph of Beryl no longer stood on the cupboard. Hudson began at once. He said:

'I wanted to see you to get some things off my chest. I've got to tell them to somebody. As you know the rest of the people concerned, you are about the only person who can give me advice.'

'I don't know about *advice.*'

'Yes, you can,' said Hudson. 'I suppose you know what I want to talk about.'

'T. T. Waring, I suppose.'

'Good lord, no. Do you mean to say you don't know what has happened?'

'Is it something to do with Roberta?'

'It is something to do with Roberta,' Hudson said. 'I suppose there is no reason why you should have guessed. The fact is, I am madly in love with her. We've seen a good deal of each other over this T. T. Waring business and—well—I don't know when it began. The other night something happened that makes it impossible for me to go ahead and marry Beryl.'

'But——'

'I won't say what it was. Perhaps you may guess. Anyway, I can't and shouldn't go through with it.'

'Have you told her?'

'I went round there yesterday.'

'How did she take it?'

'Beryl?' said Hudson, speaking deliberately. 'I suppose as well as could be expected. Very well, really. She saw pretty early on that it was inevitable. As soon as she realised that, she tried to manage things so that I looked as little of a cad as possible.'

'You mean she broke it off?'

'Actually.'

If he felt any sentiment in the matter, Hudson showed

133

none. His real life, of course, was lived among the shimmering domes and minarets of T. T. Waring's Orient, where all the men were brave and all the women, with the possible exception of Roberta, chaste. Hudson had the happy gift of detaching himself absolutely from his immediate past.

'After all,' he said, 'this may seem a rotten thing to do. But at least it leaves us both free. It would be a damned sight more rotten to get tied up together under the circumstances.'

'Naturally. If you feel that way.'

'What I wanted to ask you is this: you've known Roberta Payne quite a long time, haven't you?'

'Ages.'

'Do you think she would marry me?'

'Marry you?'

'Why not?'

'It was just rather a surprise your suggesting it.'

'I suppose you don't think I'm good enough for her. Of course I'm not. I know that.'

'It is not a question of whether you are good enough. It is a question of whether you are rich enough, tough enough, and prepared to resign your commission.'

'You think if she accepted me I should have to send in my papers?'

It was difficult to express in a few words how silly all this was. There seemed to me not the slightest likelihood that Roberta would for a moment consider becoming Hudson's wife. On the other hand, she had evidently taken a fancy to him. They might turn out to be admirably suited to each other. The silliness seemed to lie in Hudson's romantic view of her; but this might be the very factor which would make their marriage a success.

'I don't think Roberta would care to spend the next ten

years of her life in huts on Salisbury Plain and furnished rooms in garrison towns.'

'She might if she were in love with me.'

'True.'

'On the whole you don't think so?'

'I haven't thought about it at all. I had been meaning to ask you how your conversations about T. T. Waring were getting on. As we didn't meet I had no opportunity to do that. Now you tell me you have fallen for her. God knows what stage you have reached by this time.'

'But do you think I have a chance?'

'Not much.'

'I do.'

'That sounds satisfactory.'

'At least I'm not certain.'

'The only possible way of finding out definitely is for you to ask her.'

'That is what I am going to do. Before we go under canvas.'

'What! are you going camping with her?'

'Annual training is in August.'

'Sorry. No offence meant.'

'So I may get married in September anyway.'

'Let me know your luck.'

I was travelling towards Chelsea in a bus some days later when a series of little coughs and agitations from the other occupant of the seat drew my attention. It turned out to be Miss M'Kechnie, who was sitting next to the window and had chosen these methods of making her presence known. She was at once ashamed and defiant at being caught using this form of conveyance.

'I think one ought to take buses sometimes,' she said, 'it keeps one in touch.'

We both held threepenny tickets in our hands, so that it was necessary that friendly communications should be established. I mentioned that we had not met since Hugh's dinner-party.

'It was so enjoyable,' said Miss M'Kechnie, 'in spite of the coffee. What a charming child Miss Payne is. It was a very pleasant dinner, only I think Mr. Judkins is being a little silly.'

'Do you think he ought to use a percolator?'

'Not about his coffee'—Miss M'Kechnie gave that very thin laugh which she had perfected—'though there is certainly room for improvement there. I mean about Miss Payne. He brings her to all our sittings.'

'I heard that he had taken her to one or two.'

'More than that, I am afraid. You know, she has a strong influence over him.'

'Do you think so?'

'At his age, I mean.'

'But he is not as old as all that.'

'No,' said Miss M'Kechnie, drawing herself up in her seat and speaking like a blast of air from the Arctic floes, 'he may not be as *old as all that,* as you call it. But if he continues his association with Miss Payne I should not be at all surprised if he lived to regret it.'

She had taken the reference to age as a deadly insult. We were still a long way from the Town Hall, so relations had to be patched up somehow.

'But isn't Roberta interested in the sittings?'

'She seems interested in a way,' said Miss M'Kechnie, 'interested in the same sort of way that Mr. Judkins is interested. She sneers.'

Miss M'Kechnie's tone implied that this was a great deal worse than not being interested at all. She said:

'Mr. Judkins got quite angry with me the other day when

136

Mr. Pemberthy sat on the other side of Miss Payne instead of her being at the end of the row where Mr. Judkins usually arrange for her to sit. In the end he insisted on Mr. Pemberthy changing places with me on some trumped-up excuse.'

'But why?'

'Why?' said Miss M'Kechnie. 'Why? Because he did not want Mr. Pemberthy to hold her hand. That was why.'

'He couldn't be so silly.'

'He is a very self-willed man,' said Miss M'Kechnie, 'and he doesn't realise where all this is leading. The arguments he has with people are terrible. Especially about religion.'

'He has always liked arguing.'

'It has never been like this before. Not as long as I have known him. And Miss Payne is to blame for everything.'

'I think you are being rather hard on her.'

Miss M'Kechnie began making preparations for leaving the bus half-way down King's Road.

'I think people are going to have a surprise,' she said, 'if something I hear about Mr. Judkins and Miss Payne is true.'

'What?'

Miss M'Kechnie shook her head and smiled.

'No, I won't tell you,' she said. 'It would not be fair to them if it just turned out to be gossip. If it is true, there are people who will get a great shock. Some will be disappointed in Mr. Judkins.'

I moved out of the way to let her pass. There was a controversy while she tried to force the conductor to stop his vehicle at an inopportune point near Smith Square. The bus drew up some distance further on than was convenient to her. Miss M'Kechnie climbed out and walked away, trembling and muttering a little to herself.

I rang up Hudson the following week in order to catch

him before he went into camp. It was likely that I should already be abroad by the time he returned. I wanted to tell him that we should probably not meet again for a couple of months. Although we had not known each other long, I liked him enough to feel some concern at the mess he had got himself into. Besides, I was to some extent responsible for the circumstances in which he now found himself. His proposal to Roberta might or might not have taken place. It was impossible not to be curious as to the result. Hudson's voice on the telephone gave nothing away.

'Look here,' he said, 'when do you start for France?'

'The last week in August.'

'You're going to Toulon with that guardee, aren't you?'

'Bromwich is there already. I shall stay at the pub for a bit and see how I take to it. If I don't like it I shall move up the coast or come slowly home through Provence.'

'I suppose you would think it butting in if I were to come too?'

'Good heavens, no. But I thought you had other plans.'

'Could you make it the first week in September instead of the last in August?'

'I don't see why not.'

'It's like this,' Hudson said. 'I shan't be seeing Roberta again. Anyway, I don't think she had much more to tell me about T. T. Waring. I can't find out anything about him in England. I thought I might as well have a rout round France. I can use the leave that was to have been my honeymoon.'

'So Roberta wasn't playing?'

He did not answer for several seconds. Then he said:

'You know I told you I was going to ask her to marry me?'

'Yes.'

'I went round there to do it. Before I had time to get to

138

the point she told me she was going on a cruise during August.'

'Why not?'

'She said she was going to be taken by a man.'

'That sounds bad.'

'Who do you think it was?'

'How on earth should I know?'

'Judkins.'

'Who is he?'

'Hugh Judkins. Your chief.'

'What?'

'So I couldn't very well ask her to marry me after that.'

This was the explanation of the improvement in Hugh's temper that had been noticeable during the last day or two. He was taking Roberta to Scandinavia.

'But Hugh is frightfully respectable as far as women are concerned. He was a schoolmaster for ages. You will probably find the party is heavily chaperoned.'

'It isn't. She is going with him alone. She told me as a tremendous joke.'

He sounded upset when he said this.

'If she thought it was a joke, surely that is all right?'

'It isn't all right for me,' Hudson said. 'Thank God I found out before I made more of a fool of myself.'

'You mean, you never said anything about it at all?'

'I just waited until she finished talking and said I'd suddenly remembered I'd got some work to do.'

'Wasn't Roberta a bit surprised?'

'I don't know or care. But can't we fix up this trip?'

'I'll let you know dates and trains and prices for getting to Toulon, then.'

'You must write and ask Bromwich if he minds my coming.'

'He'll be quite happy about that.'

'No, you must write and ask him. I can't possibly come otherwise.'

'All right, then.'

There was nothing more to be said. When Hudson rang off I wrote to Eustace and told him that Hudson would be coming with me. I gave him no details because they seemed too complicated. A postcard with a Toulon postmark arrived some days later inscribed with the words *Abyssinia* (*both*).

7

AUGUST passed slowly. The weather was warm and damp. Now that everyone was away I managed to get some work done on *Stendhal: and Some Thoughts on Violence.* Judkins & Judkins had been promised this study for publication when finished. After three years the second chapter, 'Laughter is Power', remained uncompleted. They would have to wait patiently. Meanwhile Hugh's strictures on the publishing trade, although patently sprung from his being crossed in love, had sown the seeds of discontent. The idea rankled in my mind of getting back into advertising, where the people were worse but made more money. I wrote a couple of letters making enquiries about a new agency which was employing some of the copy-writers who had been in my former business.

Hugh had gone off on his holiday in a state of extreme nervous excitement. He looked worried but at the same time pleased. For three or four days before leaving he had answered at random any questions put to him on the subject of work. He explained everything by saying that he would leave a typewritten list of instructions. When he was gone he was found to have locked up this list in his drawer and left out on the table an important document he had intended to put in the safe. During the following week several letters sent off by him in his own handwriting were returned on account of his having put them in wrong envelopes. These and other manifestations showed that he had something on his mind.

I should have liked to see Roberta before she sailed, to find out what line she was taking about the situation. No one seemed to know her whereabouts. She was thought to be staying with friends in the country. It looked as if she would not appear again in London until the day when she was to begin her trip with Hugh.

Hudson came back from camp at the end of the month. He looked better than he had done at the time we had last met, when he had said that he was going to propose to Roberta. He was thinner and the sun had burnt his face red. He said that he had taken a lot of exercise.

'Do you think Bromwich will take us out in that boat of his?' he said.

'It will be difficult to avoid.'

'I'd like to do a bit of sailing.'

'You can bank on it.'

He seemed to have recovered fairly well from what must have been an unpleasant emotional jar. At first I thought he was not going to refer to Roberta. Then he said:

'There is one thing I should like to get straight. Just because this has happened with Judkins I don't want the fact that I am writing about T. T. Waring to be affected. After all, work has nothing to do with personal matters.'

'There is no reason why the book should be prejudiced.. I still think you are taking the fact that Hugh and Roberta happen to be on the same boat too seriously.'

'I don't want to discuss it,' he said. 'All I want is that I should not have to see her again. I can go on with the book as if nothing had happened.'

'There is absolutely no reason to prevent that.'

'Good. That is all I wanted to know.'

'Does Roberta realise that you have decided to cut her out of your life?'

Hudson thought for a moment.

'No,' he said, 'I suppose she doesn't.'

'You didn't say anything to her when she told you that she was going on the cruise?'

'I just said that I hoped she would enjoy it, and picked up my hat and walked out of the house.'

'So she knows that you are not best pleased about something?'

'She knows that all right,' Hudson said. 'But I must be going now. I shall see you tomorrow morning.'

'Victoria, 9.45.'

We arrived at Marseilles after a night spent in a steaming second-class carriage. In the north a chilly drizzle had beaten against the windows of the train and the inside of the compartment was at once hot and draughty. The other occupants were widows and commercial travellers, France's vast floating population who journey nocturnally to economise. Before settling down to sleep there had been a general movement to put on bedroom slippers and eat things out of brown paper parcels. Hudson had watched this with mistrust. There had been a change of personnel at Avignon and a quarrel about somebody's straw hat. Towards dawn I went to sleep. When I woke up my legs and back ached as if I had been put to the torture. Hudson seemed to have risen above the discomforts of the journey. He was looking out at the palm trees and white houses.

'I am going to enjoy myself here,' he said.

He was in better spirits than he had been since we had left England. The journey seemed to have cleared away some of the litter that was weighing him down. As a traveller he fussed about small matters but was prepared to endure serious hardship without grumbling. Perhaps I had misjudged his admiration for T. T. Waring as boy-scout romanticism; and really he was well equipped to share his hero's enterprises.

At Toulon there was a lot of sun and a breeze from the sea. The interior of the railway station appeared neatly arranged as for the opening act of a musical comedy. Sailors with white trousers and red pom-poms in their caps wandered about pointing at Cocteau's latest on the bookstalls, or watched the engines puffing up and down the line. Some Tonquinese infantrymen in khaki were entraining for the Buddhist temple at Fréjus. Overgrown blacks from Senegal, with their waists pinched in by red cummerbunds and wearing high tarbooshes on their tiny heads, leant against the wall, finding perpetual amusement in the antics of the French. A captain of Spahis in a scarlet tunic, baggy trousers, and a long cloak strode up and down as if he were about to sing the first number of the show.

In this crowd, and looking very much part of it, stood Eustace in a dark blue blazer with brass buttons. We climbed out on to the platform. Eustace took one of the bags.

'Come along,' he said. 'I've got a car outside. I'll run you along to the pub. I expect you want some lunch.'

We followed him to an incredibly battered Citroën standing outside the station.

'What sort of a journey did you have?' Eustace said, grinding away at the self-starter. 'Did you make any nice friends?'

'Awful. How is the boat?'

'She is in dock at the moment at St. Etienne undergoing repairs.'

We crossed the dusty square edged with palm trees and drove down towards the sea. The car bumped and rattled and groaned under the weight of three of us and the luggage. Hudson yawned. He said:

'I'm going to spend the afternoon in hoggish slumber. That old woman with the poultry kept on digging her elbow into me in the night.'

'We may as well lunch at the hotel,' Eustace said. 'Then you can both totter upstairs. We can meet later at a café.'

The Hôtel de la Mer et des Amiraux was a narrow building looking on to the port. It was approached from a street along the centre of which there was just room for a single tram-line. The manager, an etiolated Corsican, was standing at the door. He bowed low. Eustace introduced us.

'Mes amis,' Eustace said.

'Enchanté, Monsieur le Colonel.'

'Ils sont en vacances,' said Eustace. 'Quelquefois les vacances sont nécessaires. Même pour moi qui suis si fort.'

'Oui, Monsieur le Colonel.'

'Mais il faut travailler,' Eustace said. 'Il ne faut pas bâtir les châteaux en Espagne.'

'En effet, Monsieur le Colonel.'

'He's hopeless, that chap,' Eustace said. 'I can never get a rise out of him.'

We went up the stairs. Our rooms were on the top floor facing the sea. A balcony ran along in front of them. Down on the right was the Naval Arsenal. A row of awnings below on the left covered the cafés and restaurants along the quay. There were some dingy warships anchored in the harbour.

'I am in the front room on the floor below,' Eustace said. 'Do you want to unpack now or after lunch?'

'After lunch.'

We had something to eat in the dining-room on the ground floor. The food was not specially good, but the rough wine revived us a little. After the meal Hudson stretched. He said:

'I could sleep the clock round.'

145

Eustace said:

'I leave you to unpack and have your sleep. Let's meet at the Café de Sévastopol at about half-past five. It is about half-way down the quay.'

'All right.'

Hudson and I went upstairs.

'If I'm still snoring at half-past five,' Hudson said, 'don't wake me. I'll be along some time before dinner.'

'And the same goes for me.'

He went into his room and shut the door. I unpacked a few things, closed the shutters to keep out some of the sun, and lay down on the bed. The vibrations of the train had in some way communicated themselves to the mattress. The room seemed filled with people talking and arguing. There were also farmyard noises and engines shunting. After a time the irregular throbbing became dimmer and sleep descended.

When I came to, heavy breathing was still audible from Hudson's room. This was an opportunity to tell Eustace how matters stood: to prevent him from making too many jokes about Roberta in Hudson's presence. I left the hotel alone and walked down the port to the Café de Sévastopol. Eustace was at a table there reading the *Continental Daily Mail*. I sat down and tried to explain to him some of the things that had recently happened to Hudson.

'So Roberta was the cause of all this trouble, was she?' Eustace said. 'Well, I'm not surprised. And now you say she is cruising the fjords with your boss?'

'That's the official account.'

'And young Hudson has lost both his girls?'

'It looks like it.'

'He's a nice boy. I'm glad you brought him out here. We might have some fun.'

146

'The information was to prevent you making a lot of dirty cracks about Roberta. But there's another thing. He has come here to find out anything he can about T. T. Waring.'

'Oh yes, you told me Waring died somewhere near Marseilles.'

'T. T. Waring was Robinson.'

'What do you mean?'

'Robinson was one of T. T. Waring's *noms de guerre*.'

'So *that* was who he was,' said Eustace. 'I thought there was something fishy about that bird. I shall be able to make a claim on the T. T. Waring estate for my two hundred francs.'

'It's not quite as easy as that. We've only got Roberta's word for it at present.'

'What has she got to do with it?'

'She says that she was engaged to T. T. Waring—in his character of Robinson.'

'Roberta engaged to T. T. Waring?'

'So she says.'

Eustace listened to the story of this interlude.

'But what do you want to do?' he said. 'It doesn't seem to me to matter tuppence whether Robinson was T. T. Waring or not.'

'It does if you are writing a book about him. If Hudson can find out who Robinson was, he may be able to find out who T. T. Waring was. At present that is wrapped in mystery. Anyway, it will give him something to do while he forgets about his love-affairs.'

'Ah,' said Eustace, 'you don't forget. When you have been married as often as I have you will learn that. "For each man kills the thing he loves." Do you believe those words?'

'I don't know.'

'Anyway, we'll do what we can for him.'

'Why do you think Roberta is carrying on like this?'

'I suppose she took a fancy to Hudson while she was having her business conversations with him.'

'In that case, why has she gone off with Hugh Judkins?'

'Shall I tell you?' said Eustace. 'The answer is so simple that you and your clever friends would never be able to guess it in a million years. She wanted a free holiday. Poor old Judkins won't get anything out of it. I can promise you that.'

'I suggested that to Hudson. He wouldn't hear of it.'

'That's just like some chaps,' Eustace said. 'There he was, engaged to a girl who suited him down to the ground. He meets a bit of hot stuff like Roberta and breaks off his engagement. Then he expects the hot stuff to behave like the girl he was engaged to. "The coward does it with a kiss, the brave man with a sword," as I was saying.'

'He certainly went off the deep end.'

'I was just like that when I was young. Full of ideals.'

'I don't believe it.'

'Slow horses and fast women,' Eustace said, 'they were my downfall. It's annoying this boat of mine being out of action. How long are you going to stay?'

'I've got three weeks; Hudson a bit longer, I think.'

'It looks as if she won't be ready while you're here. If Hudson stays on he may have a chance of going out in her.'

'He wants to do that.'

Shortly after this Hudson turned up. He looked absurdly English in his tweed coat and flannel trousers.

'Well, old boy, did you have a good round of golf?' Eustace said. 'You look like an advertisement for what smart men are wearing in the country this year.'

'Why, what's wrong?' said Hudson.

He was not yet accustomed to Eustace.

148

'The first thing you've got to learn, young man, is to go to a decent tailor. There is one three doors up patronised by the *matelots*. You will parade at eleven o'clock tomorrow morning. The adjutant will see you properly fitted out.'

'Eustace has been hearing what you've come out here to look for.'

'About Robinson?' said Hudson.

'Yes.'

'Where was his flat?'

'Do you see that line of buildings bordering the port on the left?' said Eustace. 'It was at the top of one of those. Most of them are warehouses.'

'I must go and have a poke round tomorrow,' Hudson said. 'I think I am going to like this place.'

We used to breakfast at about ten in one of the smaller cafés on the port. Then we boarded the paddle-steamer which rocked and jerked its way backwards and forwards across the harbour to Les Sablettes, past rusty destroyers on which laundry flapped in the hot wind. Sablettes was a *plage* two or three miles by land from the town, where a deserted casino stood half-way down a flat length of shore. The paddle-steamer, which did a circular trip, unloaded its passengers at a jetty not far from this stretch of sand.

There was a wooden restaurant at the near end. Between this building and the sea the French clustered. The younger ones in bathing-dresses yelled and kicked inflated bladders backwards and forwards, sometimes, but not often, splashing into the shallow water. Bearded men in black suits, and the ubiquitous widows, created nests for themselves in the sand with newspapers, picnic-baskets, shawls, and bottles of red wine. These little groups of four or five would open an umbrella to keep off the sun and face inwards towards the centre of their circle as if they were engaged in secret rites. A policeman in white ducks armed with a pistol roamed about preserving the decencies. The most difficult of these to maintain was the regulation against men exposing the upper half of their bodies. Further along, where the beach was almost empty for a mile or so, the municipality's excessive delicacy in this matter could be disregarded, because the gendarme's white trousers were visible at a great distance. On the occasion of his rare tours of inspection along the whole length of the front there was plenty of time to assume the top of a bathing-dress.

We used to go to Sablettes most days. After bathing we had beer and sandwiches made with great hunks of French bread at the restaurant. Eustace's boat was still undergoing repairs, so there was no sailing. Eustace had infected Hudson with his interest in this activity, and there was now a lot of conversation between them about jibs, spinnakers, Brixham trawlers, and Bermuda rigs. After lunch the paddle-boat, packed with nuns, children, and middle-aged men in straw hats, took us back. The rest of the afternoon was spent by Eustace and myself in reading or sleeping. Hudson used to work at his book.

In the evening there were cinemas and *bals musettes*. We used to dine at a restaurant out by the walls on the east side of the town. Eustace said that this place was open only at certain times during the year. If you could get in there the food and wine were always good. It was approached through the *quartier réservé* along narrow streets, the high, dirty, greenish houses of which were closely shuttered. The sound of mechanical pianos churned out from the middle of the afternoon until dawn. This part of the town was like Limbo. No traffic crossed the cobbles. There was scarcely a sign of life except the distant hurdy-gurdy music. Now and then droves of sailors loafed along, arguing about money, and pausing to read the posters, torn and peeling off the leprous walls, invoking patriotism and comradeship in no uncertain terms. Later the picket prowled, a brace of Senegalese with fixed bayonets under the command of a corporal, all as black as night and wearing steel helmets. Here too the decencies must be preserved. Sometimes a door would open and a being like a decayed housemaid in a brown bathing-dress would look out for a moment and slam the door again. Over all hung the bitter smell of sea-water.

'It gets me down,' Eustace used to say, 'having to tramp past these cat-houses on the way to dinner every night.'

The restaurant was on the far side of the quarter. It was just a hole in the wall in the Italian style with a bead curtain hanging in front of it. Beyond the curtain was a deep cave with chairs and tables on either side. The food was cooked at the far end over an open fire. There was not much choice, but what there was (and the wine too) was always excellent. We usually drank a white burgundy: a Goutte d'Or, I think. The place was never full. Naval officers with their mistresses dined there, a melancholy man with a spade-shaped black beard, various friends of the proprietor, and once a minor German royalty, who had come across Eustace on some boundary commission at the end of the War, introduced a White Russian general and a Hungarian painter with whom he was sitting.

Hudson spent a lot of time making enquiries about Robinson. No one was able to tell him more than what he had heard from Eustace. Robinson's flat on the port, let again, was now used to store furniture. The concierge could give no information. Robinson had gone off one day with all his portable luggage, which was not much. He had never come back. His few pieces of furniture were worth nothing. She had taken charge of them and was using the bed herself. His rent had been paid ahead, so no one bothered about his disappearance. Hudson seemed to be enjoying himself too much to worry about this lack of data. He worked hard at the parts of the book which did not so much concern T. T. Waring's origins. Although he sometimes complained of inconsistencies in the Waring material, he reported always that he was making good progress. He never mentioned Roberta or Beryl. In fact, he seemed to have forgotten all about them.

In the few months that he had been at Toulon Eustace had made his room at the Hôtel de la Mer et des Amiraux look as if he had lived there all his life. It was full of boxes, clothes, novels, newspaper cuttings, sailing-tackle, photographs, and French comic papers. There was nowhere to sit except on the bed, because every available inch of space was taken up with Eustace's belongings. These included a bust of Voltaire which he had picked up cheap, a Second-Empire general's cocked hat, and an illustrated edition of the memoirs of Casanova in about fifteen volumes. The place looked like a second-hand shop the owner of which could not make up his mind whether to sell clothes or curios.

Hudson and I were in this room one evening waiting for Eustace, who was trying to find a clean pair of trousers. He was going through a cabin-trunk to do this. He continually lighted on treasures like the headmaster's letter to his father, asking that he should be removed from school; the cases containing his foreign decorations; or the revolver of the Turkish officer who had shot him through the leg, all of which had to be shown to us. From this collection of objects of interest he pulled a dog-eared book in paper covers.

152

'Here is a relic of your friend Robinson,' he said. 'On one of my visits made in the hope of recovering my two hundred francs I found him not at home. This was lying on the table. I took it away with me as I wanted something to read.'

He threw the book across to Hudson.

'What's it about?'

'It is written by a Swiss who went to Mecca some years before the War.'

'T. T. went to Mecca,' Hudson said.

'I expect this book gave him the idea,' Eustace said. 'It's extraordinary that I should like reading travel books so much and yet never be able to get on with Waring's. I've tried more than once. It can't be done.'

'We've had all that out before,' Hudson said. 'Some people can't. You know my views on the subject. After all, I shouldn't be writing his life if I didn't hold them.'

He took the book and began to turn over the pages.

'T. T. seems to have annotated this,' he said. 'It should be interesting. I'll chuck it into my room as we're going out now.'

'Can I see the book?'

Hudson handed it to me. It was written in French and published in Geneva. Many of the pages contained pencil notes. Some passages were scored out or had 'exp' or 'trs' marked against them.

'I wish I read French better,' Hudson said. 'Still, I expect I'll get something out of it.'

'Here are those pants,' Eustace said. 'Now we shan't be long.'

We went to a film after dinner and got back to the hotel at about a quarter to twelve. Hudson said:

'I think I'll have a look at that book about Mecca when I get back tonight.'

He used always to read in bed before going to sleep. Sometimes I could hear him creaking about for an hour or more, opening and shutting books and dropping them on the floor. That night the wind got up a bit. The shutters of the window rattled and woke me up. As I looked at my watch and saw the time was nearly half-past two I heard Hudson grunt, put down his book on the cupboard by the bed, and switch out the light. He must have been reading since midnight.

The next morning Hudson came into my room before I had finished dressing. There was no doubt from his face that something had gone wrong.

'Look here,' he said, 'that book about Mecca that Bromwich gave me.'

'What about it?'

'It is nothing but a hash-up of the T. T. Waring book on the same subject.'

'But it was written about twenty years before.'

'Exactly.'

'How can it be a hash-up then?'

'I'm going to tell you.'

'Let's go and have breakfast. Tell me on the way.'

'No. I want to tell you here. You see, it is all very well that T. T. Waring's first book should be nothing but a crib of another book on Ceylon, written sixty years ago. That might be laughed off. But now that it turns out he copied all his stuff about Arabia from a book in French, things are pretty serious.'

'You mean, all his books were produced that way?'

'It looks damned like it.'

'What do you propose to do about it?'

Hudson crossed to the window. He stepped out on to the balcony and remained there for a time looking out towards the sea. This was a disturbing discovery to have made for T. T. Waring's publishers. For Hudson himself it struck at the whole roots of the T. T. Waring legend that meant so much to him. After a few minutes he returned to the room.

'Waring seems to have lived in this town in the character of Robinson for some time,' he said. 'I thought I would go to the public library and get out some books on spec. I'll see what they have got on Cochin China, for example.'

'It is going to be a pretty bad business if the whole lot of them turn out to be faked.'

Hudson did not answer. We went along to breakfast. The radios on the quayside were already blaring away:

'J'ai vu-u . . .
Une petite femme toute nu-e . . . toute nu-e.'

Afterwards, when Eustace and I were preparing to catch the boat for Sablettes, Hudson said that he was going to explore the Bibliothèque Publique.

'What has happened to him this morning,' Eustace said, as we crossed the bay. 'Is it Roberta again? You know, I like that girl, but she has a lot to answer for.'

We bathed and lay about in the sun and had lunch. When we got back to the hotel Hudson was still out. Eustace retired to have a sleep. I went up to my room to write some letters and to re-read *Armance*. It had occurred to me that Octave shared his physiological disability with that other apostle of violence, Mr. Hemingway's hero of *The Sun Also Rises*. There might be something interesting there. While I was trying to trace further traits in common between the two unfortunate young men there was a knock on the door. It was Hudson.

'Well?'

He came into the room and sat down on the bed. This evening worry had made him look more than ever like an Englishman in a French caricature. His moustache bristled, and buck teeth, a feature never noticeable in London, showed for a moment under his upper lip.

'Did you discover anything?'

'Quite enough.'

'What?'

'I found a book about Cambodia that was an obvious foundation for the T. T. Waring volume on that part of the world.'

'In fact, he did it all the time?'

'I suppose it is only a question of tracing the origins of the remaining ones.'

Hudson got out his pipe. It was empty and he held it in his fist. The illusion was complete. He was John Bull in *Le Crapouillot*. He said:

'You see, he was always clever about it. He chose books that for some reason or another were unlikely to be translated. Or, like the first one, in no danger of being reprinted. Then he just told the story in his own words, with the philosophic stuff added.'

'What are you going to do about it?'

'What on earth can I do? Obviously I can't write the book now that the whole thing turns out to be a fake.'

'You might show him up.'

'I don't expect I should be very popular with your firm if I did that.'

This was true. The T. T. Waring books would continue to sell for some years to come. The subject, with its implications of fraud, was certainly one to be left alone by the house of Judkins & Judkins. Even if the story was built up into one of those literary exposures that appear from time to time, it would have to be a sort of book that Hudson

156

was wholly unsuited to write. The scandal might fill the papers for a week. It was not the kind of thing to interest the public, except in so much as they might cease to ask for the works of T. T. Waring at the libraries.

'Besides,' said Hudson, 'I don't feel like that. I started off with a lot of enthusiasm. I don't want to end up with a nasty little snarl. Anyway, who'd believe it? No one would bother to re-read the books and compare paragraphs. They would just go on reading T. T. Waring and say I was crazy.'

'They might. I suppose you won't go on trying to trace the originals of the other books now?'

'I may go to the public library again for my own amusement.'

'Do you want Eustace to know about this?'

'I'd rather you kept quiet about it. Anyway for the moment.'

'Let's go out and have a drink, then.'

We found Eustace in his room reading *Détective* and smoking a short black cigar. He said:

'Would you two boys like to come over to St. Etienne with me tomorrow? I want to see how the boat is getting along.'

'How far is it?'

'About forty miles. It is quite a nice little place. We might lunch on the way. You'd better take your bathing things. I don't expect I shall have time to bathe, as I want to have a long talk with the old chap who is seeing about the boat.'

'I'm not sure that I will come,' Hudson said. 'I think I'll stay here.'

'Oh, no, come on.'

'I don't think I want to.'

'A blow in the car will do you good.'

In the end Hudson agreed to come with us to St. Etienne. But he said nothing to Eustace about his latest discovery on the subject of T. T. Waring.

Toulon is always cooler than the country round about. Outside the town, on the road that runs along the sea, the sun's glare was intense. Eustace's car made painful wheezings. After travelling some distance the leather of the seat felt as if it might burst into flame; but it was a pleasant drive in spite of the heat. We had lunch at Bormes, and took a long time over it, so that St. Etienne was not reached until well on into the afternoon. Eustace found a place to park the car and we strolled down to the port.

The town stands shut off from the sea by a tongue of land, which forms a bay surrounded by rocky cliffs which are red along this part of the coast. The heavy blocks of yellow houses with slit windows look more African than French. The cafés were full of people from Montparnasse recuperating from the effects of sitting up too late. We wandered about for a time. Then we went with Eustace to see his boat.

Negotiations and discussions about this vessel showed signs of occupying several hours. Although Hudson showed interest in the subject, he decided that he would come and bathe in preference to hearing matters thrashed out to a conclusion. We arranged to meet Eustace at a café furnished with square wooden painted furniture facing the harbour, not far from a bronze statue, green with patina, representing an eighteenth-century admiral in a wig.

Hudson was morose. He spoke no more about the T. T. Waring question. As an escape from this he had surrendered himself utterly to his new preoccupation with sailing.

'That's a nice little craft of Bromwich's,' he said once or twice. 'I wouldn't mind running down the Trades on board her one year as he suggested.'

'You'll probably have a chance to sample her while you are here.'

We found a place on the beach by a breakwater, and bathed. As usual, the Mediterranean was too cold to stay in for long. Hudson did not care for lying in the sun, so we went to the café some time before Eustace was due to arrive there. From here we watched the boats moored in the harbour. Most of them were small and had coloured sails. There were two or three motor-yachts. One of these, an expensive-looking affair called the *Amphitrite,* all white-and-gold, was flying the red ensign. I drew Hudson's attention to this.

'A red ensign can be used by any Britisher,' he said. 'You or I or anyone who had a boat of our own could fly a red ensign.'

'I strongly object to the expression "Britisher".'

'Then the white ensign means a member of the Royal Yacht Squadron.'

'I know.'

'If it is a blue ensign with a device on it the owner belongs to some other yacht club.'

'A social outcast, in fact.'

Hudson took no notice. He was bent on imparting his information. He could be stubborn in matters of this sort.

'The Royal Naval Reserve use a blue ensign,' he said. 'So do vessels maintained under the Colonial Defence Act.'

'You're telling me.'

There is no knowing how long he would have continued on this subject if his attention had not been distracted by a man who appeared on the deck of the white-and-gold yacht. This figure stemmed for a moment the flow of nautical lore. The man was small and dark. He wore a béret and a dashing pair of bell-bottomed trousers. He was standing with his hands in his pockets at the top of the gangway, looking up and down the quay as if he wanted to make sure that the coast was clear before he ventured ashore. Apparently he was satisfied with the outlook because he came slowly down the gangway and towards the café. He had an unusual walk, half-swaggering, half-cringing, like a comedian's on the stage. Hudson, with a strange expression on his face, stared at this figure.

'What have you seen?'

Hudson did not answer. The man reached the front of the café, glanced at us, and made for a seat at the back, passing on the way close by our table. As he did so Hudson put out his hand and touched him on the arm.

'Hullo, Alec,' Hudson said.

The man in the béret turned round slowly as if he expected to see something highly unwelcome to himself. Whatever he feared, the sight of Hudson was a relief. His face brightened up at once. He said:

'Why, Tiger? Fancy meeting you here. I didn't recognise you at first.'

'It's a bit of a surprise, isn't it?'

'Where are you staying?'

'Toulon.'

There was an awkward silence. Having brought this situation on himself, Hudson was not entirely capable of dealing adequately with it. He sat fingering his glass, flushed in the face. The man called Alec looked in my direction. Hudson said:

'This is Alec Pimley——'

'Alec Mason now,' said the man in the béret quickly. 'I changed my name after I broke with my family. Do you mind if I sit down?'

160

Hudson muttered something about my knowing the Pimley family. Alec Pimley, now that he had recovered from his first surprise, was absolutely at his ease. He said:

'So you know my people?'

'Yes.'

'Have you known them long?'

'I used to go over there to tennis when they were on Salisbury Plain.'

'Ah, then.'

Close up, his face was lined as if he had been through a good deal. He had that open, appealing frankness of expression of those who live by their wits. There was a touch of pain in his eyes as if he felt that life had treated him with injustice. He said to me:

'If you know my family you probably know that I was a bit of a black sheep. We won't go into all that now. What is past is past. When I married I decided to take my mother's name by deed poll. You quite understand, don't you?'

'Quite.'

It was a curious question to ask.

'And you, Tiger?'

'Yes, of course,' said Hudson, grunting with embarrassment. 'I didn't know you were married. When did that happen?'

'I haven't been married long. Only a few months. You must meet my wife. If you stay here a few minutes you will, because she is joining me in this café for a drink before dinner.'

'Do you live at St. Etienne?'

'We are living on the yacht at the moment,' said Alec Pimley. 'We are on our way to the Greek islands.'

'Whose yacht is it?'

'Ours.'

'Yours?'

'Yes.'

Hudson seemed to regret ever having reintroduced himself to his old school-friend, who, in spite of his remarks about leaving the past undisturbed, was evidently determined to talk about himself.

'I expect you've heard all sorts of pretty putrid things about me, Tiger,' he said. 'Well, I dare say a few of them are true. I hope you didn't believe all of them.'

'No,' said Hudson. 'Only some.'

Alec Pimley shouted with manly laughter.

'Good old Tiger,' he said. 'You always knew more about me than I did myself.'

'What happened after you left the East?' Hudson said soberly.

Alec Pimley closed his eyes for several seconds. Then he said:

'I knocked about a bit. Then I decided to settle on this coast. I had friends here, you see.'

'But what did you live on?' said Hudson.

He had a downright way of asking questions that even an old-timer like Alec must have found it hard to side-step. At least, his answer did not come out quite so pat this time. He said:

'A bit of journalism here and there. A good deal of poodle-faking. People don't mind springing a tenner now and then if you can make yourself useful to them. And then the generality of mankind are good-hearted folk.'

That phrase seemed to have a ring I knew. I had an idea Hudson himself had used it recently.

'They never seem to want to spring one for me,' Hudson said.

Alec Pimley clapped him on the back.

'Tiger,' he said, 'you'd have done yourself in long ago

162

if you had had to swallow some of the things I have. But, as you know, I am a tough nut.'

Hudson said nothing. To hear them talking one might have thought that he had failed in life and Alec Pimley's notable success gave him the right to be a shade condescending to an old and less fortunate friend. This patronage, so gently implied, was edging Hudson by perceptible degrees into a weak position. No doubt Alec Pimley's life had been spent in establishing this relationship between himself and the people with whom he came in contact.

'And so you've come out here for a holiday?' he said. 'Do you like it?'

'Very much.'

'Going up for the Staff College soon?'

'I've thought about it.'

'I think you'd make a good staff officer, Tiger.'

'Thanks.'

'Ever see either of those two sisters of mine?'

'Sometimes.'

Alec Pimley's voice took on a richer tone. He said:

'Do you know, Tiger, it used to be a sentimental dream of mine that you should marry Beryl. Funny the way one plans things of that sort when one's young, isn't it?'

He put his head on one side and fixed his eyes on Hudson, who stirred uncomfortably.

'Did you ever think of it?'

'I was engaged to her, as a matter of fact.'

'You don't mean to say she broke it off?'

'It was my fault,' Hudson said. 'I behaved like a cad. I expect you may have done something caddish once or twice in your life, so no further explanations will be necessary.'

'Oh, my dear Tiger, I am so sorry.'

Alec Pimley looked really concerned. His small features

took on a worried, foxy expression that for a moment recalled Beryl's face. His eyebrows were like Winefred's. Apart from this, he did not much resemble either of his sisters. He put his hand on Hudson's shoulder. He was about to say more when he was interrupted by a voice behind us. It was an American voice.

'Why, here is Alec, Captain Bromwich. And he has found your two friends.'

A woman in beach pyjamas was standing by the table. Eustace was close behind her. She was elderly and her face was familiar. But wherever I had seen her before, she had not been wearing red trousers. Beneath her floppy straw hat some grey hair was visible, incredibly well cared for. In fact, her whole appearance showed that she spent a lot of money on looking as smart as possible. At the back of my mind some memory of her stirred. It was something to do with a darkened room and people I knew well.

Eustace stood in the background with an expression on his face that might have been the outcome of any strongly felt emotion—rage—laughter—disgust—pity—or just boredom. He bowed formally to Alec Pimley and introduced Hudson and myself.

'I don't think you've met Mrs. Cromwell,' he said. 'You will remember that nice Rolls-Royce of hers that I drove over the precipice.'

'But I'm *not* Mrs. Cromwell any longer,' the woman said; 'I am Mrs. Mason now.'

'For me,' said Eustace, 'you will *always* be Mrs. Cromwell.'

'But you mustn't forget that it was you who introduced me to my husband, Captain Bromwich.'

'He was called Robinson then,' said Eustace. 'I am a simple soldier. I cannot keep up with these aliases.'

Mrs. Cromwell shrieked with laughter. Alec Pimley, whose eyes had become uneasy, began to look less apprehensive now that he saw his wife treating everything Eustace said as the funniest joke she had ever heard in her life. Hudson gave no sign that he had absorbed the revelation that Eustace's words carried with them. It was, so to speak, the end of Hudson's pilgrimage. If Alec Pimley was Robinson he must also be T. T. Waring. If he grasped the significance of this author's various incarnations, Hudson did not choose to make immediate use of his knowledge. It was even possible that he was still mystified. Eustace had pulled up a chair for Mrs. Cromwell and she sat down next to me. Before there was an opportunity to tell her that we had met before she began to talk.

'Isn't this little place great?' she said. 'Look at those old houses and the old boat and the old man over there. Do you see them all? Thank you, I will have a manhattan. Garçon, un manhattan.'

'You know, Bromwich,' said Alec Pimley, 'there's something I want to remind you about. I've thought of nothing since we last met but that two hundred francs I owe you.'

'They've given me some sleepless nights too,' Eustace said. 'I suppose you don't happen to have them on you now? They would come in very useful. But how on earth did all you boys get together?'

'Tiger is an old friend of mine,' Alec Pimley said. 'We were at school together.'

'What?'

'I never told you I was at a public school,' said Alec Pimley with a sad smile, 'did I?'

'You didn't have to,' Eustace said.

Mrs. Cromwell, who had been drinking in the beauties of the middle distance, said:

165

'It seems a crime to come to a little place like this and spoil it all. Don't you feel ashamed when you look at those old fisherfolk? Don't they make your life a pretty cheap concern?'

'You can't have it both ways,' said Eustace. 'If we didn't come here we shouldn't have met. You've just been saying how pleased you were to see me again.'

'And I should say I am pleased, Captain Bromwich. It does my heart good.'

At that moment Mrs. Cromwell's drink arrived. This took her attention. She sipped it and made a grimace.

'Now, why do they tell me they can mix a manhattan if they can't?' she said. 'It is just as easy to speak the truth. If they had been honest about it I could have drunk Pernod. But, no, they have to say they can mix a manhattan. Why do they do it? I put that question to you.'

'It was a preposterous drink to order,' Eustace said.

His line with Mrs. Cromwell, the line that had caused her to want him for a husband, was evidently extreme severity. On this occasion, however, she was too incensed about her drink to take any notice of him. The proprietor of the café was standing close by, having a chat with a swarthy female friend. Mrs. Cromwell thumped on the table.

'Mais par exemple, Monsieur le Patron, il faut faire les cocktails avec le whisky Canadian Club. C'est le meilleur whisky pour les cocktails manhattan, vous savez.'

'Have something else, dear,' said Alec Pimley.

Eustace's arrival was something he had not bargained for. His voice was querulous. He seemed to have no plan of campaign.

Mrs. Cromwell said:

'No. I will not have something else. But I know just what we will do. We will go and have a nice drink on the

166

Amphitrite. Why ever did I not think of that before?'

Her husband did not like the suggestion at all.

'Don't forget that we have got to dine early tonight, dear,' he said.

'Why, whatever——'

'We have got to dine early,' he said. 'And, anyway, I don't think I want another drink. And I am sure that you don't either. You know what the doctor said about your acidity.'

'Personally,' said Eustace, 'I should love a drink on your yacht, Mrs. Cromwell. There is nothing I should like better.'

Mrs. Cromwell was delighted.

'That is just like your charming way, Captain Bromwich. Why, dear Alec, I am ashamed of you. It looks so inhospitable to talk that way.'

Alec Pimley seemed to have decided that his earlier geniality had not been what was required. It had let him in for too much. He said:

'I think I shall stay here. Of course I am delighted for you to see the yacht. In fact, one of the reasons I don't want to come with you *now* is that I want to keep my talk with Tiger about old times for when he comes and dines on board. If I come with you now and start yarning with him and having more drinks we shall be late for dinner.'

Mrs. Cromwell said:

'Sometimes I can't understand you at all, Alec. But let us all go and leave Alec there.'

The effect on her of remarriage and the south of France had been prodigious. The coffee and lemonade provided at the séance in Kensington seemed a part of her life she had entirely blotted out. We got up from our chairs. Suddenly Hudson said:

167

'Alec is right. There are lots of things he and I want to talk about. Some of them won't take long. You two go and see the yacht. If you come back in about twenty minutes Alec and I will have had our talk.'

'As a matter of fact,' said Alec Pimley, 'I've got some things to buy in the town——'

'Never mind,' Hudson said, 'I'll come with you. There is something I particularly want to ask you.'

'But you will see me again. You must come and dine next week. The fact is——'

'This won't wait,' Hudson said.

It sounded a little as if he planned to commit murder.

'Why, if you won't come, Captain Hudson,' said Mrs. Cromwell, 'I shall be disappointed. But of course we shall meet again.'

'I'm awfully sorry,' Hudson said. 'I must seem rude.'

'Not rude,' said Mrs. Cromwell, with one of those old marquise smiles. 'Just a good friend.'

'That's it,' Hudson said. 'Just a good friend.'

He raised his hat. Eustace and I followed Mrs. Cromwell towards the white-and-gold yacht. Hudson and Alec Pimley remained at the café. When I looked back from the top of the gangway they were already engrossed in their chat about old times.

We went below into a saloon done up as a bar in a style of quite unusual hideousness. Mrs. Cromwell rang a bell. A young negro appeared. She told him to bring some drinks. Eustace with his hands in his pockets walked round the place inspecting the fittings. It occurred to me that Mrs. Cromwell had not yet been reminded that we had met before.

'I don't expect you remember me. I came to your house

in London once. It was with Hugh Judkins. The night Mimi mentioned T. T. Waring.'

'You came to that sitting?'

'Yes.'

'Why, of course you did,' Mrs. Cromwell's voice rose until it became almost a squeak. 'Now, I _knew_ we had met before. And was not Captain Hudson there too, brought by Mr. Lipfield? I thought he was. Now isn't that a coincidence? And how is Mr. Judkins and that sweet girl his fiancée?'

'His fiancée?'

'Maybe she isn't his fiancée. The one he used to come with to the sittings. Why, she is the sweetest, prettiest young thing.'

'Roberta Payne?'

'That is her name.'

'She is very well as far as I know. But I had no idea there was any question of their getting married.'

'I dare say there is not,' Mrs. Cromwell said. 'But these things happen so quickly. One never can tell.'

'So you two know each other?' said Eustace, coming to a standstill between Mrs. Cromwell's chair and the bar.

'We met,' said Mrs. Cromwell, 'soon after a turning-point in my life. I married Alec secretly. He had insisted that I should come back to England for a short time while he cleared up certain matters in France.'

'How soon did you get married after I introduced you to each other?'

'It was not long,' Mrs. Cromwell said. 'Alec certainly spoke up at once. Do you know, Captain Bromwich, I had such a strange feeling the moment I set eyes on him.'

'There's something about him,' Eustace said. 'Isn't there?'

'Oh, yes,' said Mrs. Cromwell, 'I should say there is.

169

Anyway, we got married. And then there were these business affairs that Alec had to put straight. He said they would just worry me if I was on the spot, so back I went to London. To tell the truth, there were a lot of things I had to get done myself. You can't ever enjoy yourself without having to pay for it. In trouble, I mean.'

She sighed. It was to be presumed that she was thinking of the camp-followers in the world of psychical research whom she had had to pay off. These, no doubt, were the rows Lipfield had spoken of when we had met in the City.

'Then we bought the yacht,' she said, 'and I came out and met Alec in Corsica. Now that he's married he says he's gotten a distaste for the French coast. We only looked in here at St. Etienne because I wanted to see some old friends who were staying in the hotel for a day or two. Alec was all against it. But I insisted.'

'So Alec left Toulon as soon as he got married?'

'He said he just could not stand that place one moment longer. He gets like that. I never know where I am with him. Now tonight he says that we have got to dine early. But why we have to dine early I have *no* idea.'

'When do you sail for Greece?' said Eustace.

'Tomorrow,' Mrs. Cromwell said; 'but it must be put off. We must meet again. I shall call you up at your hotel. Where is it?'

'The Mer et Amiraux, Toulon. Look here, may I see over your yacht? I'm mad about boats of all sorts.'

'Why, certainly, Captain Bromwich.'

'We ought to be getting back soon,' I said, 'oughtn't we?'

Anything might have happened in the café. I did not know whether Eustace realised the state that Hudson must be in by this time. He might let himself in for the guillotine

170

or Devil's Island. Since Eustace had insisted on seeing the yacht in the face of such discouragement from Alec Pimley, it looked as if he had deliberately intended to give Hudson an opportunity to have it out with Alec about the T. T. Waring question. If so, he appeared to think they had still not had enough time together.

'We will see over the *Amphitrite* first,' he said.

Mrs. Cromwell took us round. She seemed to regret that all chance of persuading Eustace to marry her must now be at an end; but as this was impossible she could congratulate herself on having made a satisfactory compromise. Eustace tapped and tested everything. There was no doubt that the boat must have cost a lot of money.

'Do you ever hold sittings here?' I asked.

'Now that I am married I shall have to give up my psychical research. Alec does not approve of it.'

'On what grounds?'

'He did not tell me just what the grounds were,' said Mrs. Cromwell. 'But when I began to tell him about some of the very interesting experiences we had had with Mimi, he let me get to where she gave us that wonderful warning about T. T. Waring and then he took my hand and said: "Darling, I want you to give all this up. I don't think it is right." '

'And so you are not letting Lipfield and Miss M'Kechnie and the others foregather in your house again?'

'I am afraid I shall not be able to,' Mrs. Cromwell said. 'And besides, some of the people you meet are very disappointing. You would not believe how I have been disappointed by mediums.'

'Will you be coming back to London soon?' Eustace said.

'Alec doesn't like London so very well either.'

'But you won't be staying here?'

'We'll be cruising around,' said Mrs. Cromwell, 'cruising around. Maybe we shall stay at Corfu for a spell. But should we be getting back to Alec now, or he will be sore because he wants to dine early? Though what he wants to do it for I can't say at all.'

Hudson and Alec Pimley were still sitting at the café table. They could be seen from the top of the gangway. Mrs. Cromwell waved to them. Alec Pimley waved in return. I saw him get up from his chair and hold out his hand to Hudson. It looked as if he took both of Hudson's hands in his when he said good-bye. The distance was too far to see for certain whether or not this was so. Then he came slowly in the direction of the yacht.

'I shall call you up tomorrow morning at your hotel,' Mrs. Cromwell said. 'I shall have to talk over the change of plans with Alec first. Then we will arrange when you can come and have supper.'

We said good-bye to her and went down the gangway. As Alec Pimley came nearer, his face showed that nothing fatal had happened so far as he was concerned. He looked flustered, but pleased with himself.

'I hope my wife has arranged when we are to meet again,' he said. 'I want to have a chin-wag with old Eustace again.'

'She's going to ring us up to-morrow,' Eustace said. 'I say, old boy, you've hit it pretty rich, haven't you?'

Alec Pimley gave his melancholy smile.

'Fortune's wheel,' he said. 'Good-night.'

He walked up the gangway.

'The bastard,' Eustace said.

We went on to the café. Hudson was sitting with his legs stretched out in front of him. Eustace said:

'The question is: where are we going to have dinner? Here or at Toulon?'

'Let's go back to Toulon,' Hudson said. 'I've had enough of this town.'

'What did you say to him?' I said.

'I'll tell you some other time,' Hudson said. 'What could one say to that sort of creature?'

We found the car and began to drive west. Eustace said:

When I knew that fellow he hadn't got a sausage. Not a sausage. And now he owns a boat the size of the *Titanic*.

Hudson, who was sitting in front, did not answer.

'It's amazing,' Eustace said. 'Could either of you two do that? Marry a woman for her money and own a boat that size. I don't believe I could do it.'

We were going at about fifty. Suddenly Eustace slowed up to thirty-five.

'My God,' he said.

'What is it?'

'I never got my two hundred francs.'

'But we're going to see him again.'

'I'm not taking any risks this time,' Eustace said. 'I've learnt wisdom.'

He drew in at the side of the road. Then he turned the car. We set off again in the direction of St. Etienne.

'You can't do this, Eustace.'

'Can't I?'

Hudson did not seem to care what happened. He sat looking straight ahead of him on the seat beside Eustace. I was hungry. It looked as if we should have a late dinner by the time Eustace recovered his money and we got back to Toulon. The heat had abated now. The wind was getting up a bit and was blowing the sand across the *pavé* of the quayside as we arrived back in the town. Eustace stopped the car and switched off the engine. He looked up towards the sky.

'There will be a storm tonight,' he said. 'I know just how they blow up on this coast. It's not the sort of night to be on the water.'

He turned towards the sea. A white yacht, flying the red ensign, was sailing towards the mouth of the little harbour.

'Look!'

As he watched, a large drop of rain fell on the wind-screen. It splashed smaller drops in a circle over the front of the glass. Eustace said:

'You're quite right. It certainly is. Master Robinson is a quick mover. I wonder what he told Mrs. Cromwell we had done that persuaded her to slip her moorings so smartly.'

We sat there until we saw the yacht disappear round the bend of the mole.

'I'm sorry to have brought you back for nothing,' Eustace said. 'It is going to be pretty wet on the road to Toulon. But if you take my advice we shall do it at once rather than later.'

Rain was now falling heavily. We put the hood up as quickly as possible, but not before the inside of the car was fairly wet.

'That's good-bye for ever to my two hundred francs,' Eustace said. 'I shall enter it tonight in that fat little volume, the Book of Bad Debts.'

The sea looked like a stretch of worn tarpaulin. Jagged black clouds were blowing up from the other side of the town. Hudson's face was the colour of whitewash. He hardly spoke on the notably unpleasant drive back to Toulon.

That night there was a storm. The rain, blown by the wind first in one direction and then another, swept across the harbour. The awnings of the cafés on the port flapped and crackled. Some masonry crashed down from the direction of the Naval Barracks. It was impossible to go out in this tornado. We had a late meal in the hotel. After dinner we played cut-throat in Eustace's room with the jalousies creaking and rattling all the time as if the building was going to collapse. At last Hudson, who had been silent all the evening although he had won consistently, said that he was going to bed. Eustace, who always liked sitting up late, suggested a game of piquet. I was tired and refused.

'Very well,' Eustace said. 'It is no good for me to try and get to sleep yet. I shall hang about until this din subsides.'

'If you wait till then you'll wait all night,' Hudson said.

'Good-night, you cheerful devil,' said Eustace. 'I shall read my Claud Farrère.'

He put the cards back into their box and picked up *L'Homme qui assassina*. Hudson followed me upstairs. When we arrived on the top landing he came into my room.

'Incredible, isn't it?' he said.

'Pretty odd.'

'Alec of all people.'

'What did you say to him?'

Hudson took a deep breath.

'I simply taxed him with being T. T. Waring,' he said. 'He didn't attempt to deny it. Of course he was surprised that I had been commissioned to write the life.'

'Did you tell him how much you liked the books?'

'Yes. He seemed pleased about that.'

'He offered no explanation of his conduct?'

'Only the need to earn a living.'

'But why did he kill off T. T. Waring?'

'When he married there was no more need for him to

175

make money that way. Mrs. Cromwell has settled some on him.'

'It would have been easier just to fade out.'

'He thought that if he established as a known fact that T. T. Waring no longer existed there would be less likelihood of a fuss if the truth ever came out.'

'How did he rig it?'

'He sent a cable in the name of an American journalist he knew, announcing the death to a New York paper. That started the ball rolling.'

'And all the books are cribbed from one source or another?'

'Yes. As Judkins said that night we dined with him, there is nothing in the world the public like so much as reading the same book over and over again.'

'You didn't threaten to expose him?'

'I began blustering. He just asked why I should want to break up his life now that he was happily married. And added that if I did anything of the sort I was going to look a pretty good fool myself.'

'I see.'

'I suppose he is right.'

'So he will get away with it?'

'Yes.'

'He didn't say why he took the name of Waring?'

'He did, as a matter of fact. He got it from a poem by Browning. Apparently it had always made a great impression on him as a child.'

'What a boy!'

'I'm not going to stay here after this,' Hudson said. 'I can't stick it.'

'But there are only a few days longer anyway. Why go before I do?'

A flash of lightning shot across the room. The thunder

clattered immediately after. The electric light went out; and then on again. Hudson said:

'I'll sleep on it and see how I feel in the morning.'

He went out and into his own room. Instead of going to bed he must have sat down and tried to think things over, because it was an hour or an hour and a half later that I heard him bumping about angrily while he undressed.

The next morning the air was cooler than it had been since we had arrived in the south. The weather had cleared up. The awning was ripped away from the café where I found Eustace having breakfast. The waiter said that a lot of damage had been done at the Arsenal. Water still dripped from walls and broken gutters. Eustace said:

'That was a God Almighty storm last night.'

'It certainly was.'

'Did Tiger give you the works about this T. T. Waring business before he went to bed?'

'I heard some of his views on it.'

'I thought you would,' Eustace said. 'I didn't discuss it. After all, it doesn't involve me at all. I thought he wouldn't want to dish it all up with two other people.'

'He is rather upset.'

'I can't see any point myself in kicking up a lot of fuss about a beachcomber who has made good.'

'He talked about going back to England at once.'

'What I can't understand,' said Eustace, 'is why, having discovered a good way of getting a steady income, Robinson, or Pimley, or whatever his name was, thought it necessary to marry old Cromwell. He must be a very luxury-loving young man.'

'He did not make as much money as all that.'

'What do you suppose he used to knock up?'

'I don't expect it averaged much more than four or five

hundred a year. He had to produce pretty well a book a year for that.'

'But the books were all written by other people.'

'Even so, he had to adapt them and write in the uplift.'

'But I thought he was a best-seller?'

'He sold very well. But he wasn't making a fortune.'

'You disappoint me,' Eustace said. 'I was thinking of writing my recollections. Now I shan't.'

There was still no sign of Hudson. We walked back to the hotel. I went up to his room and knocked on the door.

'Entrez.' He sounded gloomy.

Hudson was sitting on the bed. He was resting apparently from packing, which was in full swing.

'Look here,' he said, 'I'm going back. Do you mind?'

'Of course not, if you want to. But why not stay the few remaining days?'

'I want to be alone,' he said. 'I thought I'd have a look at Arles and Avignon on the way back. You don't think it's letting you down, do you? There's Bromwich. Anyway, it is only the matter of the inside of a week.'

'Not if that's how you feel.'

'I suppose I was a fool ever to get mixed up with the whole affair from the start,' he said. 'It really isn't my line.'

'No one could possibly have guessed how it would turn out. You can hardly have been more surprised than I was.'

'It's different for you. You never thought the books were any good. I did.'

'It was a very ingenious fraud.'

'What the hell does that matter?'

'It matters a lot to me. I admire Alec Pimley far more than I ever did T. T. Waring.'

'I can't understand you at all,' Hudson said, beginning to fold up the dinner-jacket which he had insisted on bringing with him. 'The thing is a fake, and there is an end of it.'

'Well, we are going over to Sablettes. Are you catching the evening train?'

'Yes.'

'We will be back in time to see you off.'

'It's not only the book,' he said; 'there is my mucking things up with Beryl. It is all part of the same business.'

'Why don't you try and patch it up with her?'

He stood in the middle of the room, folding the evening trousers into a small compact parcel. When he had done this he put them in the suitcase before he answered. At first I thought he was going to agree that a reconciliation would be the best thing for both of them. He said:

'It's not much of a story to have to tell a girl about her brother.'

'I don't expect she has many illusions about Alec by this time.'

'And then she would see what a fool I was to be taken in.'

'She wouldn't mind that.'

'I can't,' he said; 'I simply can't. Not after what has gone before.'

'Why not try?'

'It just couldn't be done.'

'I think you're a fool to say that.'

'That is your business.'

There was just time to catch the boat for Sablettes. Eustace was already on board.

When we returned, Hudson was waiting in the Café de Sévastopol. He seemed more collected than he had been earlier in the day. He was apologetic about leaving.

'I've always wanted to see the Papal Palace,' he said;

'and those Roman remains. I've read about them, you know, but it is nice to see things for yourself.'

'When do you want me to bring the car round for your baggage?' Eustace said.

'I've taken it round to the station already,' Hudson said. 'I thought I might as well do that when I bought my ticket.'

Later in the afternoon we went with him to the train and saw him off. In the end he seemed quite sorry to leave. Eustace insisted on giving him a sample bottle of Vieux Marc to help him through the night.

'See you in London' were Hudson's last words.

Eustace and I walked back across the dusty square. 'I think,' said Eustace, 'he will soon be owning one of those vessels which are described as rubber, handleless, lunatic officers, for the use of.'

'I shouldn't wonder.'

'How did he get in such a state?'

'T. T. Waring and Roberta Payne.'

'And yourself.'

'I suppose so.'

A boy passed selling *Le Petit Provençal*. Eustace had a pathological urge to buy any periodical he saw exposed for sale. He took a copy.

'Let's rest here for a while.'

We sat down in a café on one of the corners of the square. It was getting hot again. Eustace studied his paper.

'This storm seems to have done the hell of a lot of damage,' he said.

'Read out any funny bits.'

'What about this? *Crime odieux d'un Quinquagénaire.*'

'Was that the result of the storm?'

'No; he thought it up last week.'

'Go ahead.'

Eustace read the passage, translating as he went.

'Anything more like that?'

'Do you want to hear *Un ouvrier métallurgiste a abattu sa maîtresse d'un coup de couteau?*'

'Use your judgment.'

Eustace continued his running commentary.

'What a banal story.'

Eustace folded up the paper and put it in his pocket. He said:

'The more I get married the more sure I am that it is the natural state for men and women. I shall begin looking round again. I have been without a wife for too long.'

'Have you anyone in mind?'

'I have my lists at home,' Eustace said. 'Let's go back to the pub. I want a sleep before dinner.'

I returned to England about a week later.

8

In London things were much as usual. There was, however, a letter from the advertising agency I had approached before going abroad which held out some hope that they might need my services. At present they could promise nothing. Something more definite in the way of answer would be sent in a week or two. It looked as if my days with Judkins & Judkins might be numbered. In the used-up atmosphere of late summer even the prospect of more money was not specially stimulating. As usual after coming home from the Continent, I felt that the only acceptable restorative would be a long holiday.

My desk at the office had been tidied. The galley proofs of *Lot's Hometown* lay on the blotting-paper waiting for correction. A pile of manuscripts to be read stretched unevenly into the distance like Hadrian's Wall. The authors, those middle-aged women in the Midlands, East-Anglian clergy, Scotch students, Indian Civil Servants, and the rest, all finished their novels in August. They sent them off to a publisher at the beginning of September. There were at least eighty of them waiting for inspection. This was surprising, because Hugh had been at work for more than a fortnight. He was accustomed to deal summarily with the stuff that had accumulated while he was away. Bernard was still in Scotland staying with relations.

When I went down to Hugh's room he was sitting at his table reading a small black book like a hymnal. As he looked up I had the impression that some change had taken place in him since he had gone away. His appearance was healthier than it had been for a long time; but his eyes had sunk back into his head. They were brighter than they had been before his holiday. He smiled with an assurance that he had never carried in the past. It was as if he had put a weight off his mind at the price of a great sacrifice.

'Good-morning.'

'Good-morning to you,' Hugh said.

'Did you have a nice cruise?'

'A very nice cruise,' Hugh said, still grinning.

Sooner or later he would have to be told about T. T. Waring. There was no reason to rush such information. It must not come as a shock. Besides, Hugh's new manner made it advisable to approach such a subject with caution.

'There seem a lot of manuscripts waiting to be dealt with.'

'They can all go back,' Hugh said. 'I don't know why I have not sent them back before.'

That at least was a relief.

'Is there anything good in at the moment?'

'One or two very hopeful things,' Hugh said. 'A better type of thing altogether.'

He held up the little black book.

'I'll hand this over to you when I've finished it,' he said. 'I think it will interest you.'

'I see the proofs of *Lot's Hometown* have come in. Shall I go through them?'

Hugh's face clouded over. He closed the little black book, marking the place with a paper-folder.

'I have been thinking about *Lot's Hometown*,' he said. 'I have come to the conclusion that we cannot publish it.'

'But it is already in proof.'

'It is a book I never liked,' Hugh said. 'I have given orders for its publication to be postponed indefinitely.'

183

'The author or his agents will have something to say.'

'Some other publisher can take it from the printer at advantageous terms. We do not want to handle muck like that.'

Hugh was breathing heavily. He had worked himself up all at once into an extraordinary state of excitement. So far as I could remember, it was Hugh himself who had read a review of the book in an American paper and had suggested sending for it. Bernard had never liked it. The only explanation of this volte-face was that the novel was to be abandoned as a concession to Bernard and that Hugh was feigning disgust to save his face.

'What sort of a time did you have in France?' Hugh said, with the tone of one who changes the subject deliberately.

'A lot of things happened. Shall I tell you about them? It is rather a long story.'

'Go ahead.'

Hugh showed little or no interest in the narrative of events from the discovery of T. T. Waring's plagiarisms to the revelation that he was Alec Pimley. He behaved as if he was having someone's dreams described to him. Halfway through the chronicle I began to wonder if he were even listening. At the end he said:

'So T. T. Waring was a fake from start to finish?'

'Yes.'

'And he is now married to Mrs. Cromwell?'

'Yes.'

'And he always has been a *mauvais sujet*?'

'Yes.'

'I am not surprised.'

'But I thought you admired him so much.'

'I used to. Now I see more clearly.'

'It was a great disappointment to Hudson.'

'Hudson should turn his mind to more serious matters. I

184

don't know why he wanted to meddle with writing at all. It wasn't his avocation. He should stick to his last.'

Hugh had often shown contradictory moods, but this was something out of the ordinary run of caprice. That he should hear of the exposure of his favourite author with approval showed that something radical had changed his point of view. It looked as if Roberta might be at the bottom of this. At the same time it was hard to see how even she could have brought about such an apostasy.

'By the way, are you doing anything special this evening?' Hugh said.

'I am, unfortunately.'

I was going round to see Roberta after dinner. I had arranged this before coming down to see Hugh. I thought that he was going to suggest my assisting at another séance.

'That's a pity.'

'Not another sitting by any chance?'

'No,' said Hugh, and his voice almost broke with the force he put into it. 'I'm finished with all that.'

'Oh, really?'

'The Truth is not there.'

And then he laughed abruptly as if he had not meant to speak in so serious a tone.

'You know, I've always thought it was a lot of rot,' he said; 'and at last I decided that it was too much waste of time to go on with. I wanted to ask you whether you had ever heard of the Sons and Daughters of the Tabernacle.'

'I can't say I have.'

'They are rather an amusing little sect. They happen to be holding a meeting tonight. I thought we might have dropped in.'

I suppose I must have looked so surprised that Hugh felt some further explanation was necessary. He said:

'I have become interested in some of those little cults

185

recently. You know, there is a lot in some of them. This particular one is run by a very intelligent fellow. He is a retired lieutenant-commander, as a matter of fact.'

'But what do you do at them?'

'I like attending their services,' Hugh said. 'It broadens one's outlook. They very flatteringly asked me to give an address one evening. I said I couldn't tie myself down about that.'

'I should like to be present if you ever decide you will speak.'

'You must certainly come some time,' Hugh said.

He spoke quickly while he was telling me about his new hobby. It was just the way he used to refer to his Spirits. He seemed to see nothing exceptional in the idea that he should get up and speak at a conventicle.

'So there is nothing special for me to read?'

'Have a look at this.'

He threw across a tattered bundle of manuscript. I glanced at the title page. It was an account of missionary work in the Pacific.

'It looks as if a good many people have seen this before us.'

'Never mind,' said Hugh. 'They are sometimes the best sellers. Anyway, it is the sort of thing we want. More in keeping with the original traditions of the firm.'

I took the manuscript up to my room.

When I had arranged to see Roberta, who had a right to hear about T. T. Waring at the first opportunity, she had said that she had a lot of things to tell me.

'I have some news for you too.'

'I'm sure it is not as strange as mine.'

'I am sure it is.'

After interviewing Hugh I could almost believe this; but

186

at the time it had seemed to me that her budget of information could not possibly rival my own. There was, accordingly, some likelihood that she would be able to throw light on the change that had taken place in Hugh.

Roberta lived in a mews not far from Belgrave Square. It was nicely done up in white with Regency furniture. Someone had given her a small Sickert to hang over the mantelpiece. It was easy to imagine Hudson's fall in such surroundings. The outside was painted bright yellow. Roberta herself opened the door. She was looking well after her trip and very pretty. I had not seen her since the night of the Territorial dance.

'First of all,' she said, 'I must tell you about *poor* Mr. Judkins—or Hugh, as I really call him now—though Mr. Judkins suits him so much better. Have you noticed anything about him since he came back?'

'He is distinctly odd.'

'That's what I mean,' said Roberta. 'I can't understand it at all. It happened while we were away.'

'What did?'

'Well, you know Mr. Judkins was kind enough to suggest that I should come for a cruise with him up the Scandinavian coast?'

'I gathered that.'

'Of course,' Roberta said, 'it was rather an extraordinary thing to suggest. One could not possibly have done it with anyone less reliable than Mr. Judkins—don't laugh, I mean it. In fact, he did say that we might try and get Miss M'Kechnie or someone to come too. I said I thought it would be far more fun if it were just us. You see, by the end of the summer one always feels a bit of a wreck. I thought a nice quiet healthy holiday away from all the people one knows would be such a good thing.'

'What a sensible girl you are, Roberta.'

'Aren't I? Well, this idea seemed to please Mr. Judkins very much, so off we started. At first it was very nice. I thought I had been quite right about Mr. Judkins, who behaved himself perfectly. We both got very brown and healthy and frightfully Scandinavian. And then one day he suddenly asked me if I would marry him.'

'That always seems to be happening to you. Was Hugh after your money too?'

'I was really rather embarrassed,' Roberta said. 'You see, it was very sweet of him to take me on the cruise and all that, but naturally I did not want to marry him. I had to tell him so.'

'How did he take that?'

'He said he knew it had been no good asking. He was rather melancholy and romantic. I tried to be as nice as possible about refusing. I thought it would all be forgotten. But the whole thing seemed to have unsettled him.'

'What happened?'

'The next day his manner changed completely soon after lunch. He suddenly asked me if I had ever read a short story by Somerset Maugham called *Rain*.'

'About a missionary who tried to reform a girl from the Red Light district and then fell for her and committed suicide?'

'That's the one. I said I had, and that I thought it very good. Mr. Judkins smiled in the oddest way and said: "Has it ever occurred to you that our relationship is rather like that described in *Rain*?" '

'What did you say?'

'I said I had never worn shiny white boots in my life, and if I did my calves would not bulge over them. I said I could not imagine what he meant and I hoped he was not going to cut his throat on the next bit of beach we came to.'

'That was a very proper answer.'

'Then he said: "You know you are a harlot, Roberta, a harlot." He said it twice.'

'What frightful cheek!'

'I thought he had gone crazy. I think he had for the moment, because he began apologising almost as soon as he had said it. He never spoke like that again during the rest of the voyage, which was fortunately nearly over. It was rather awkward, wasn't it?'

'It sounds very awkward indeed.'

'But he was never the same after that. He had been quiet for some days before it happened and had spent a lot of time reading in his cabin. Afterwards he scarcely appeared at all except for meals. Sometimes not even then. But he was always the soul of politeness.'

'What do you think caused this?'

'Well,' said Roberta, 'I don't want to seem vain, but I suppose it was disappointment.'

'It took rather a drastic form.'

'I was a little reminded of a relation of mine who emigrated to America, where he started a new religion.'

'But Hugh has never shown any signs of this before.'

'There was all that spiritualism.'

'But he approached it from a distinctly sceptical angle.'

'He told me he came from a family who belonged to some unusual sect. I expect it's all bursting out.'

'That's too bad.'

'Will it affect the T. T. Waring life?'

Roberta's description of Hugh had sent the thought of T. T. Waring out of my head. She had still heard nothing of the, discoveries that had been made on this subject. I tried to give her some account of what had happened. This took a long time: but, unlike Hugh, Roberta was attentive.

'And so the book won't appear anyway?' she said.
'It can't.'
'There is no reason why I should not try to sell my stuff about T. T. Waring to some paper as a short memoir?'
'None whatever.'
'Of course one won't make much money that way,' she said. 'But I suppose it is the best one can hope for. What an extraordinary story it is. Poor Tiger.'
'Have you seen him since he came back?'
Roberta shook her head. She said:
'You know, I really rather fell for Tiger at one moment. I thought he looked so handsome in uniform at that extraordinary dance. And then he was captivating while we were having our conversations about T. T. Waring. I think I told you I like shy men. But something happened. I don't know what it was. He suddenly got offended with me. It was the afternoon I told him that I was going on this Scandinavian trip. He went off in a huff. I haven't seen him again. Perhaps it was just as well, because he is really rather a bore, isn't he? And the poor sweet is desperately serious and has no money at all.'
'That's the situation.'
'And he is going to be married to a rather dull girl, isn't he?'
'The engagement was broken off.'
'Did they have a row?'
'Yes.'
'How silly of them. He obviously ought to get married and what's called settle down.'
'That's what I think.'
'Well,' said Roberta, 'all these things are very disquieting. It only shows how careful one ought to be.'
'It does.'
'Oh, and there is something else,' she said. 'You know

190

Judkins & Judkins are publishing my collected articles. I suppose they will come out all right?'

'They are being printed.'

'Keep an eye on them, do,' said Roberta. 'In Mr. Judkins' present mood anything might happen.'

Hudson told me that he had enjoyed himself on his journey home through Provence. The amphitheatre at Arles had especially pleased him. He said that nothing much had happened but he had an opportunity to think things over and had come to various decisions.

'When I got back,' he said, 'I went to the C.O. of my Territorials and told him how matters stood. Not in detail, of course, but about my engagement being broken off and so on. I said I wanted to go back to the regiment. He was very decent about it. Said he quite understood. He even thanked me for all I'd done for them. I felt rather a swine.'

'Which battalion are you going to?'

'Wait a bit. To give up this job I have to apply to go back to my regiment. I want the time with them to be as short as possible. Or even make my return only nominal.'

'What are you going to do then?'

'I had been thinking about whether I could get seconded to the Iraq Levies or the Gold Coast Regiment or some force of that sort. Well, I ran into a fellow called Pemberthy. It was in the swimming-bath at the R.A.C., as a matter of fact. One of the Territorial officers had taken me there.'

'I suppose Pemberthy remembered meeting you at that séance?'

'When we got talking it turned out that we'd first met there. At the time he said Lipfield had introduced us at that dance. I didn't know him from Adam.'

'But what has Pemberthy got to do with it all?'

'He started off on T. T. Waring. The séance had made him very keen on Waring's books. I had to ride him off that. Then he got on to the subject of the Sudan. In the course of conversation it turned out that he had a great friend in the Colonial Office. You see, the Colonial Office are the people who could get me appointed to the sort of thing I want.'

'And has he arranged something?'

'He was splendid. I went to see his friend. It looks as if everything is going well.'

'Where would you be sent?'

'I won't mention the actual unit in case things fall through. It would be in Africa.'

'You'll be able to write a book about it.'

I did not mean to say that. It came out by accident, a piece of conversational ineptitude entirely without motive. Hudson went red.

'I think I'm finished with literature for the time being, if not for life,' he said. 'By the way, will you be seeing the Pimleys again?'

'I shouldn't think so for a moment.'

'Hasn't Beryl's father still got your stamp album?'

'So he has. I'd forgotten all about that. How am I to get it back? How on earth did you remember that?'

'I thought of it the other day,' Hudson said. 'Of course I realise that in the ordinary way you probably wouldn't meet them again. I mean, going there through me and so on. But I've found an iron Beryl lent me. I don't exactly like to send it back without saying anything. Equally I don't want to have to write to her. I wondered whether you could take charge of it and hand it back when you get the chance.'

'A flat-iron?'

'A golf-club, you bloody fool.'

'What a lovely job!'

'Well, the General is bound to get in touch with you sooner or later about the stamps. There is no hurry.'

The stamp album was an aspect of my relations with the Pimleys which I had forgotten at the time when Hudson had broken off his engagement. General Pimley had said something about going through the book at his leisure and letting me know what he wanted when I returned from abroad.

'I think he will probably send the stamps back, saying that he has not found anything he needs for his collection.'

'Is there likely to be something he wants?'

'It was a good small collection of its kind.'

'In that case,' Hudson said, 'you will hear from him. His stamps mean a lot to him. He won't miss the chance of adding to them cheaply. If he just sends the album back with a polite note you can send her the club yourself. I'll pay the postage.'

'Look here, why on earth don't you make it up with her?'

'I can't,' Hudson said. 'Sometimes I think I'd like to. But I could not tell her about T. T. Waring being Alec. It may sound silly, but I couldn't do it.'

'I think it's damned silly, if you really want to make things up.'

'It can't be helped.'

He began talking about Africa, the shooting, and what opportunities there would be for studying the natives.

'Isn't this being rather like the hero of a Ouida novel?'

'Perhaps. I suppose I'm like that. Did you tell Judkins who T. T. Waring was?'

'Yes.'

'How did he take it?'

'He scarcely seemed to notice it. He has come back from his holiday in a very strange state.'

'Why?'

Hudson had not mentioned Roberta, so I had told him none of her account of Hugh's behaviour in case the subject might be painful. It was now unavoidable.

'Apparently his conduct became odd when he was away.'

'What did he do?'

'He called Roberta a harlot.'

Hudson laughed. He had evidently recovered from his infatuation. He said:

'Well?'

'That is not the sort of way he talks generally.'

'Had she given him any cause to complain?'

'None so far as can be seen. Nor to congratulate himself either. Their relations seem to have been perfectly innocent, so that it was no business of his anyway.'

'What is he doing now that is out of the ordinary?'

'He won't look at any manuscripts unless they deal with uplift of some sort. The other day I caught him reading a tract.'

'What do you put this down to?'

'Heaven knows.'

I put down most of it to Roberta; but Hudson could not very well be told that.

'And so T. T. Waring is just to be allowed to slide?'

'It looks like it.'

'After all that fuss,' said Hudson. 'But perhaps it is just as well.'

Hudson was right about General Pimley. A letter arrived a few days later in which the General wrote that he had examined the collection, made notes of the stamps he wanted, and hoped that I would suggest a week-end when I could come down to Camberley so that he could go through the album with me. In this way, he said, I should be able to see that he was offering me a fair price. If I noticed that he had stolen any specimens I could mention the matter then and there.

I thought it polite of him to include the invitation in his letter, but that in the circumstances the Pimleys could hardly want to see me. I therefore wrote that there was no need for him to be put to this trouble. If he felt that to return the album with a cheque made the transaction too unbusinesslike he could send me a written statement of his appropriations with a list attached of current catalogue prices. I had forgotten everything of the market value of individual stamps, which must have changed considerably since the collection had been made. In any case, the sum involved could scarcely exceed two or three pounds at the most hopeful estimate.

Another letter arrived by return of post. In it General Pimley said that he would be most disappointed if I could not arrange to stay with them. In fact, he must insist that I did so—if not in the near future, then as far ahead as necessary. He added that Beryl particularly wanted to see me again. The letter ended by asking if the following week-end was by any chance open.

Hudson had handed over the golf-club he wanted to return to Beryl. Staying with the Pimleys would offer an opportunity to give it to her with the least possible fuss. If the General was so determined that his gleanings in the stamp album should be checked by the owner on the spot it was only a matter of sooner or later before I should have to go down there. The information about Beryl was mysterious. General Pimley wrote on black-edged notepaper.

.   .   .   .   .   .

Shirley Handsworth came into my office without knocking. The weather was still too warm for his camel's-hair overcoat. He was wearing a grey flannel suit on which faint mauve squares were visible at close range. His face was bewildered. It was not uncommon for Shirley to register bewilderment. When he did so, trouble was in the air. His book was getting too little advertisement or his advance had not been big enough.

'What is wrong, Shirley? You look worried.'

Shirley shut the door and came nearer. For him to enter my room, except as a matter of necessity when everyone else was engaged, was unusual. In a low voice he said.

'What has happened to Hugh?'

'Hugh? Nothing that I know of. Why?'

Shirley sat down on a chair. He brushed away his sparse black curls from his forehead.

'I've just had an extraordinary interview with him,' he said. 'I'm still gasping. I felt I couldn't go out in the street at once.'

'But what ever did he do?'

'It wasn't what he did. It was what he said. I went in to see him about some points in my autobiography, which is going along very well. Hugh suddenly began a lot of stuff about why couldn't I try and get out of the awful depths I seemed to have sunk to, and what ever was my future going to be, and now was the time, before it was too late.'

'What could he have meant?'

'How should I know? At first I thought he was joking. You know the way Hugh always hammers his jokes in rather a long time. But then he began saying all sorts of things I didn't even know he knew about, winding up with all this attack on my writing.'

'What sort of things did he say?'

'Oh, you know. Beastly things. I thought I was such a favourite with Hugh.'

Shirley sniffed. His nose was running and a shiny film appeared over his small bulbous features. He was so put out that for a minute or two it looked as if he was going to cry with annoyance. He said:

'Hugh can't expect me to go on being published by this firm if he speaks to me like that.'

'Perhaps he was feeling ill this morning. He has a lot of trouble with his inside.'

'But you don't understand'—Shirley became shrill— 'this wasn't just a touch of bad temper. It was something much worse. Hugh *hates* me.'

'He can't.'

'But he does, I tell you. He said the most awful things to me. Of course I'm too young to be a really good writer yet; but I try awfully awfully hard, and one day I may achieve something.'

'Don't talk like that, Shirley. You'll break my heart.'

'What have I done anyway?'

'Hugh has been worried lately. His holiday seems to have disagreed with him. He will settle down.'

'He went off with that girl Roberta Payne, didn't he?'

'She was on the cruise too.'

'I suppose she put him against me.'

'I'm sure she did nothing of the sort.'

'She is probably jealous of my books.'

'She can't be.'

'If it is not that, then someone else has been saying dreadful things about me. I don't know what to do. I don't think I can ever meet Hugh again.'

'You will neither of you feel so bad about it all tomorrow.'

197

'But haven't you noticed any change in him? I saw it as soon as I came into the room.'

'Hugh has been a bit off colour lately, it's true.'

This sort of thing was disturbing. It was all very well for Hugh to be eccentric in the office and refuse to read manuscripts unless they had to do with philosophy or theology. A good business might be built up on such foundations. Judkins & Judkins had made their start with books of a similar sort. But if Hugh intended to set about improving the personal characteristics of all the authors on the list, the firm would be bankrupt before there was time to effect this metamorphosis from general to specialised publishing.

'What does Bernard think about him?' Shirley said.

'He has mentioned nothing. He has only been back a day or so.'

'I shall go and see my agent,' said Shirley; 'and if Hugh asks about me you can tell him that's where I went.'

General Pimley himself was waiting on the platform when I arrived at Camberley. He was wearing a black tie.

'Taking up golf at last?'

He stared at Beryl's iron, which I had tried unsuccessfully to hide from him.

'No, it's Beryl's.'

'Oh, I see.'

He looked younger and more cheerful than when we had last met. We got into a new and larger car. As we drove along the High Street he said:

'I should warn you the house is in rather a mess. It is always the same after a death. Things take a long time to clear up.'

'I didn't see the papers when I was away. Who——?'

'My father. He was a great age, of course. In some ways it was all for the best. Coming as it did the same time as the other business, I think it took Beryl's mind off a bit.'

He cleared his throat.

'Beryl is anxious to see you,' he said. 'That was the main reason why I wanted you to come and talk about the stamps here instead of lunching at my club one day.'

'How is Beryl?'

General Pimley seemed relieved now that he had made this statement about his daughter. He said:

'A bit depressed. A bit depressed. It was a bad show, of course. Young Hudson such a nice fellow too. We are trying to arrange for her to go out for a month or two and stay with friends at Nairobi. Something like that will make her forget, you know.'

'And Winefred?'

I asked this without thinking, expecting he would say that she was all right, or no worse, or something of the sort. Instead, General Pimley frowned.

'Between you and me,' he said, 'there has been some trouble about her too.'

'Nothing serious, I hope.'

The General looked straight ahead of him. He said:

'This must go no further. We found she was engaged secretly to a most unsuitable fellow. Surprisingly unsuitable.'

'Has it been broken off?'

'It had to be. As a matter of fact, I believe he was married already.'

'Really?'

'Twice.'

'Married twice?'

General Pimley nodded.

'Two wives,' he said. 'All this is in confidence, of course. But it has caused me a lot of worry.'

'So I should think.'

'We thought it best for her to go and live in London for a bit. She has always wanted to have a job. She helps with some charities that cousins of ours are interested in.'

'And I suppose she comes down for week-ends?'

'Sometimes,' said General Pimley. 'Not this one, as a matter of fact. But I mustn't bore you with my family affairs. I am looking forward to going through the album with you. I shall want some of the imperforates, and the 1867 issue with the grille are all splendid specimens.'

We drove past bungalows and a golf-course. August had been hot, General Pimley said. In spite of the rain that had fallen in the early part of the summer there was a shortage of water. The grass looked parched. Some charred gorse marked the limits of a heath fire. The unspeakable pines gave off their medicinal odour.

'We get a lot of fires at this time of year,' General Pimley said, 'some of them too near the house to be pleasant.'

The change that had taken place at the Pimleys' was noticeable as soon as we went through the front door. A lot of the knick-knacks that had formerly littered the hall had been removed. The passage had been repapered in a lighter colour. The drawing-room chairs and sofa had been re-covered and a number of pictures had been taken from the walls. Mrs. Pimley was arranging the flowers. She showed signs of having had to endure recent stress and had lost some of her assurance.

'Beryl will be here at any moment,' she said. 'She is most anxious to have a talk with you.'

All these warnings about Beryl were ominous. Neither of her parents seemed to know what she wanted to discuss. Mrs. Pimley even showed signs of being inquisitive, as if she supposed that I knew already what Beryl had on her mind. She may have thought that it had something to do with patching up a reconciliation between her daughter and Hudson. It was unlikely that either Mrs. Pimley or her husband knew what had happened to cause the engagement to be broken off. Whatever they thought, both of them made excuses when tea was over and left Beryl and myself alone together while they went off on various errands.

Beryl had become quieter. If she had anything special to say she did not hurry to mention it.

'I've got a golf-club of yours with me. Tiger asked me to let you have it back.'

It seemed best to announce this at once in case Beryl might reveal something that made the subject unapproachable. I did not want to carry the implement about with me the rest of my life. She flushed a little at the mention of Hudson's name.

'An iron?' she said.

'I think so.'

'Leave it in the hall,' she said. 'I'll put it in my golf-bag.'

'I'll go and get it now.'

When I came back with the club she said:

'I suppose you haven't seen anything of Winefred in London?'

'I haven't.'

'You know why she went?'

'Your father said there had been trouble of some sort.'

'There was an awful row. They found out about all the business we talked of in front of you. That was why Winefred was sent to London. I'm very worried because I'm almost sure she goes on seeing the—the man there.'

'But surely he is at Sandhurst?'

'He's left there.'

'Your father said he was married—twice.'

'We thought so at first. Now it seems uncertain. It may be someone else with a similar name.'

'You mean she might marry him.'

'Yes. All this happened just at the time my grandfather died. You knew he was dead, didn't you?'

'Your father told me. I was so sorry to hear about it.'

'He was awfully old,' she said; 'it was to be expected. The point is that Father got Winefred and me to help go through his papers.'

'Did he leave a lot?'

'Piles. Most of them not of the slightest interest. That was why Father got us in to help. Box after box about sea-weed.'

'Seaweed?'

'He used to collect it when he was younger. For scientific reasons. But there were also some things I want to show you.'

'What sort of things?'

'You'll see,' she said. 'They are in the smoking-room. Shall we go in there?'

We went along the passage to the room where Captain Pimley had given me his views on Alec. Like the rest of the house, it had been brightened up. All traces of Captain Pimley's sojourn there had been removed. Beryl went to a cupboard under the bookcase. Unlocking the lower door she pulled out a papier-mâché box, also locked. The key of this she took from a vase on the mantelpiece where it was hidden, whether deliberately or not she did not say. Beryl opened the box. It was full of letters done up in packets which were tied round with tape. She took out one of these packets and handed it to me.

'Have a look at these,' she said.

The envelopes had French stamps on them. For some reason the handwriting looked familiar. I unfolded one of the letters and began to read it.

'My dear Grandfather . . . long since I heard from you . . your last ten pounds . . . living simply as I do . . .'

The letter was signed 'Your affectionate grandson, Alec.'

The address was Poste Restante, Nice. I read several of the letters. They all asked for money in the style upon which every professional begging letter is modelled.

Beryl said:

'Have you discovered what they are yet?'

'I gather they are from your brother, sponging on your grandfather.'

'You knew I had a brother, then?'

'Tiger told me.'

'Did you know before?'

'No.'

'That was why I asked,' she said, 'because a lot of people don't know. Have you got to the one where he mentions a change of address?'

'Not yet.'

'It begins: "The sea looks very blue from my window this morning . . ." '

'Here we are.'

The letter was much the same as the others. The passage Beryl pointed out came at the end.

'. . . if you could spare a small cheque, my dear grandfather, send it to Monsieur Robinson to the above address, for that is the name under which I pass here in Toulon, where I live in a very modest way, not wishing that one of our family should be known to have fallen on such evil days . . .'

'Do you see now?' said Beryl.

'Your brother used to call himself Robinson.'

'Robinson was T. T. Waring,' said Beryl. 'You know that. Or if you don't you ought to. Or rather T. T. Waring and Alec are the same person.'

'But how did you know about T. T. Waring being Robinson?'

'Tiger told me, of course.'

'I see.'

'I should have found it anyway, from the letters.'

'Does he admit it in so many words?'

'Practically. But that is not all.'

'What else?'

'In one of the letters Alec says he can never be grateful enough for Grandfather's silence about the memoirs. I don't know what that means exactly. But with the letters are two or three copies of an old book. Father saw them and said that it was a book Grandfather had written as a young man.'

'*Memoirs of a Journey in Ceylon?*'

'Why, have you heard of it? Father said he hadn't seen the book for years. He had forgotten all about it. Grandfather must have hidden all the copies of the book he had with the letters.'

'Do you know why?'

'No.'

'It was because your brother had copied most of it out to make his first book under the name of T. T. Waring.'

'But the reason that I am telling you all this is because Tiger ought to know it for the book he is writing. I want you to take the letters to him. He can do what he likes with them. Burn them if he likes. But he ought to know.'

'The rest of your family haven't seen these letters?'

'No.'

'Not even Winefred?'

'I was alone when I found them. I hid them at once.'

She did not seem specially surprised to find that her brother was T. T. Waring. Authorship is only impressive to those in the book business. All she wanted was that Hudson should benefit by the information.

'The book is off, as a matter of fact.'

'Off? Why?'

'For the reasons you have just given me. It was discovered that your brother was T. T. Waring. We met him in Toulon, as a matter of fact.'

'Who did?'

'Tiger and I.'

'Tiger was with you abroad? But how could you meet Alec? He is dead.'

I told her what had happened when we were in the south of France.

'Then Tiger is not going to write the book at all?' she said at last.

'He can't very well.'

'What is he going to do?'

'He has given up his adjutancy. He is trying to get sent to the King's African Rifles or something like that.'

'Oh dear,' she said. Then she began to cry.

Later in the evening I went through the stamps with General Pimley. This was the most enjoyable part of the visit. Mrs. Pimley seemed disappointed that nothing better had resulted from my meeting and talking with Beryl. I told them that I had to dine in London on Sunday night, and cut the week-end as short as possible.

Bernard called through on the house telephone as I was preparing to leave the office on Monday evening. It was unexpected that he should not have gone home by that

205

time. He said that he wanted to see me and I went down to his room. Bernard was sitting at his desk breathing heavily. He looked old and tired.

'I wanted to talk to you,' he said—and paused for some moments as if reconsidering this desire—'about Hugh.'

'Yes?'

'Sit down,' said Bernard. 'Bring the chair up close.'

I pushed the arm-chair across the worn carpet, leaving a trail in the dust. One of the legs buckled, but the chair did not break. It was fairly safe if you kept your weight on the left side. After we had sat opposite each other for a while Bernard said:

'Have you noticed anything about my brother since he came back?'

He said this loudly.

'He doesn't seem to have been quite himself certainly.'

'What sort of thing have you noticed? You need not fear to speak. He has left the office.'

It was like being cross-questioned by a stage detective.

'He doesn't show the same interest in manuscripts. He always seems preoccupied with theological questions whenever I go in to see him.'

'Exactly,' said Bernard, seizing on to this as if it was the clue to the whole situation, 'exactly. He is preoccupied with theological questions. Have any of the authors complained to you?'

'Not very much—at least——'

'Well?'

'Shirley Handsworth seemed cross about something.'

'What did he complain about?'

If he were prepared to listen to the story of Shirley's troubles Bernard must think things were in a very bad way.

'Apparently Hugh said that he did not care for the style

206

of Handsworth's work. He suggested that he should try something of a more serious nature.'

'Read these,' said Bernard.

He handed me three letters. All were addressed to himself. The first was typewritten and the other two were in thick illegible handwriting.

The first letter said:

DEAR MR. JUDKINS,

I cannot see what my having been divorced three times has to do with my books, but as I have had several better offers from other publishers I shall be glad to concur in the suggested dissolution of my contract with yourselves.

Yours sincerely,

Œ. GULLIVER-LAWSON.

The other two letters were from Redhead and Minhinnick respectively. They were long and querulous. It appeared that Hugh had written to Redhead, warning him that unless his next novel contained less about illicit love Judkins & Judkins would be unable to see their way to accepting it. Redhead was angry. He had written to Bernard for an explanation. Precisely what Hugh had said to Minhinnick was not apparent. The substance seemed to be that Minhinnick was an old man who would be better occupied with thoughts of the next world rather than with such vanities as the writing of an autobiography. Minhinnick was definitely angrier than Redhead.

'I take it the letter to Mrs. Gulliver-Lawson was from Hugh too?'

'You don't suppose *I* wrote it, do you?' said Bernard. 'She must have misread the signature when she answered to me. Why should I care how often she gets divorced?'

There was a long silence.

'I wanted to ask you whether you had any idea what has caused this,' Bernard said.

'It is very hard for me to say.'

'You know,' said Bernard, 'even as a small boy he was strange. Paul and I could never make anything of him. What about all the jiggery-pokery with spirits? Is that at the bottom of it?'

'He's been interested in that for a long time.'

'I know.'

'He always used to laugh about the séances.'

'That sort of thing plays Old Harry with a man,' Bernard said. 'I shouldn't wonder if that fellow called Lipfield hadn't influenced him.'

'I don't think so.'

'Do you think it was something that happened when he was away?'

'It looks rather like it.'

'Who did he go with?'

Bernard said this hoarsely. He leant forward. His bleary eyes became almost cunning.

'He went on a cruise. As a matter of fact, Roberta Payne, who was going to help with the T. T. Waring book, went on the same cruise.'

'Do you think she had something to do with it?'

'What can she have done?'

'Perhaps,' said Bernard, speaking as if he were at the same time pushing a heavy piece of furniture across the room, 'perhaps it was what she did not do.'

'Possibly.'

'And then,' said Bernard, 'this story about T. T. Waring. Hugh tells me some extraordinary stuff about T. T. Waring being a fake. Said you brought it back with you.'

'It is true.'

'We can go into that later. But whatever has happened it can't be so bad that a biography cannot be brought out about him.'

'I am afraid it is.'

'Well, I was never keen on the idea,' Bernard said, 'but Hugh thought a lot of it. Now he shows no disappointment at all. He told me this extraordinary yarn. Then said it was all for the best.'

'It is an amazing story.'

'Not only that, he says we can't publish the new T. T. Waring manuscript that came in recently from Peppercorn. Why, it is already in hand.'

Bernard sat back in his chair. He said:

'That doesn't prevent him from insisting on producing a book of collected newspaper articles from this young woman Payne just because he says he has given his word that they should appear.'

There was another long pause. It was hard to know what to suggest. Then suddenly Bernard banged the pile of weekly papers on his desk. He said in a voice that came from right down inside him:

'*This—can't—go—on.* We shall be in Carey Street before we know where we are. I shall tell Hugh it has got to stop.'

I took this to mark the end of our conversation and got up to go. While I was crossing the floor there was the sound of scrambling steps in the passage outside. The door was opened violently. Hugh walked quickly into the room.

'If you have got anything to tell me,' he said, 'you'd better say it now.'

He was white in the face and shaking a little.

'You seem very fond of saying things behind my back,' he said. 'Perhaps you would like to repeat them to my face.'

Bernard sat in his chair looking as if he were going to be sick. Hugh said:

'I suppose you think I can't hear when you make these criticisms of me at the top of your voice. Or perhaps you thought that I had left my work at the early hour you usually see fit to leave yours.'

These assaults began to sting Bernard slowly to life.

'I was only waiting to confirm certain conclusions,' he said, 'before I approached you.'

'What conclusions?'

'That we shall be bankrupt if you go on behaving in this way.'

'What way?'

'Sending letters to authors that make them write back to me in these terms.'

Bernard held up the three letters he had shown me. He fluttered them in Hugh's direction. Hugh took them from him and glanced at them. While he did this he grinned to himself.

'Well?' he said.

He handed the letters back to Bernard.

'What on earth do you mean by referring to Mrs. Gulliver-Lawson getting divorced three times?'

Hugh clenched his teeth.

'We have got to have this out sooner or later,' he said. 'Now you have raised the matter perhaps it had better be sooner. We are going to change the tone of the books we put out. We can't go on flooding the market with what is at best trash and at worst *filth*.'

'Filth?' said Bernard. 'Filth? What do you mean? And anyway, if it was, who would be to blame? Haven't I always complained that you liked sailing near the wind?'

'Never mind what happened in the past. I speak of the future.'

'I don't know what you are driving at.'

'Decency,' said Hugh, 'that is what I am driving at. It is a quality that some of the authors on our list seem to have forgotten the meaning of.'

'Being rude to them won't help them to remember it,' said Bernard.

He was getting very angry.

'It might do you good yourself,' said Hugh, 'to have a spiritual overhaul, Bernard.'

Bernard fetched a sound that gave some hint of his irritation.

'What about you?' he said; 'and this young woman you took to Norway?'

Hugh began to tremble all over. The skin of his face went quite blue. He might almost have been about to have a fit. He said:

'What do these continual efforts to insult me mean? I insist on an explanation.'

He kept on opening and closing his mouth. His halo of reddish hair, which he had somehow ruffled, stood forward on his forehead like a comb. Bernard said:

'Insult you?'

'Why did you point at me in Great Russell Street yesterday?'

'I——'

'You did. You know you did. You were walking with Peppercorn.'

'Are you mad?'

'There you go,' said Hugh, taking a step nearer to Bernard and swaying backwards and forwards so that it looked as if he were about to fall to the ground. 'Because I want to bring decency into this cursed profession which you forced me into by your own sloth, because I have begun to tire of battening on human weakness, because the things that are good seem to you less saleable than the things that are evil, because the whole edifice of your business has its foundations in the rottenness and corruption of human flesh, you see fit to point at me and make a mock of me in the public way, and, not content with this, you must add a foul and unjust libel that strikes not only at my good repute but that of a girl who—who—who——'

Hugh, whose forehead was covered with sweat, staggered to the arm-chair. He threw himself down in it. The leg, which had cracked under my weight, instantly gave way. Although the list sent Hugh heavily over to the far side of the chair he continued to sit in it, leaning forward with his head in his hands.

'Oh dear, oh dear,' he said.

Bernard stood up.

'Telephone for a taxi,' he said.

Hudson rang up the next day.

'Everything is arranged,' he said. 'I've been pretty busy. We must meet before I leave London. What about dinner tomorrow?'

'I can't manage it. The next night?'

We discussed dates. For one reason or another there was difficulty in finding an evening when we were both free. I suggested the end of the following week.

'That will be my last day,' Hudson said. 'I may have to stay down here fairly late.'

'There are some things I've got to tell you.'

Hudson thought for a moment.

'Look here,' he said, 'why not come to these headquarters for a drink? We can have a talk here. Then I'll get away for dinner if I can. If not, I'm afraid you'll have to dine alone.'

'How do I get there?'

'I'll tell you if you don't mind making the trek. It's a bit much to ask. Only I'm leaving England quite soon.'

'What are you going to do?'

'Ride a camel.'

9

THE line of approach taken by Bernard to the subject of Hugh's outburst in the office was that his brother had been overworking.

'Then he goes on a holiday and sits in the sun all day,' Bernard said. 'Naturally he gets a nervous breakdown. I don't believe in all this sun myself.'

'I suppose he is in bed now?'

'The doctor says he must stay there for some weeks,' Bernard said. 'Then he goes to Scotland. We have relatives there. The air will do him good. Poor fellow, he has always been highly strung.'

Bernard added nothing of the prospects of Hugh remaining in the business. If he thought these remote he kept his thoughts to himself. I was in a weak position for making further enquiries because I had heard from the advertising agency that they had an opening. Sooner or later the news would have to be broken to Bernard that I myself was to leave Messrs. Judkins & Judkins. Bernard, who had bought a new suit and allowed his beard to grow into a more decided point, seemed no longer worried by what had taken place. No doubt he was delighted at the prospect of getting back into his own hands the control of the business. Possibly his plans had been laid for years to cope with an eventuality of this sort.

That afternoon I set out for the Territorial headquarters. The expedition took the best part of an hour from Piccadilly Circus. It was not one to be embarked on lightly. The last lap of the journey was completed by tram. When I arrived at the gates, Hudson was walking briskly across the yard.

'Hullo,' he said, 'I'm still up to my neck in work. Come along to the Mess. I'll get you a drink. We can talk later.'

'What about dinner?'

'We might eat something at about half-past nine or ten. I shall probably be finished by then.'

'If I don't die of starvation in the meantime.'

'You can wait. It will do you good. I can't possibly get through my mopping-up and get back to London before then.'

We went up some stairs to the Mess ante-room. Hudson rang the bell.

'What will you drink?'

'Sherry.'

A depressed character in shirt-sleeves and a green baize apron appeared and took the order.

'I'll be back in seven minutes,' Hudson said. 'Make yourself comfortable.'

He went away. I examined the surroundings. The room was narrow and contained several leather arm-chairs and some small tables on which a few papers lay. There was a shiny black clock on the mantelpiece. Above this hung the reproduction of a picture by Lady Butler. The figure in shirt-sleeves reappeared, carrying a glass of sherry, and then retired through a half-open door at the end of the room. Beyond this a long table could be seen with chairs set on either side of it. I moved over to the fireplace and was making a closer study of the picture above it, which was called *Floreat Etona!*, when the door opened and some-one came in.

'Why, good afternoon.'

It was Lipfield. He marched across the room, looking as military as he could in mufti—which was considerably more military than he did in uniform—and shook hands. I explained that I was waiting for Hudson and that we were going to have a late dinner together that evening.

'And how is Mr. Judkins?' Lipfield said.

'He has had a bit of a breakdown, as a matter of fact.'

'Has he?' said Lipfield. 'That is interesting.'

'Why?'

'I had an idea something of the sort might happen.'

'What made you think so?'

Lipfield shook his head.

'I sent Mr. Judkins one of the usual notifications of a sitting some weeks ago,' he said. 'We hadn't seen him for some time as he had been away. The letter that arrived back would have surprised you.'

'What did it say?'

'What didn't it say? I've known Mr. Judkins in some strange moods but never like this. I didn't answer it. I saw there must be something wrong with his health.'

'Did he say he disapproved?'

'That is exactly what he did say,' said Lipfield; 'and he put it in a nasty way too. But I won't talk any more about it. He couldn't have been himself. I expect he will write to me when he is better. But when are we going to have the pleasure of your company again?'

'You promised you would invite me one day.'

'Did you tell me you were not going to dine with Captain Hudson until half-past nine or ten?'

'Yes.'

'Then why don't you come to Miss M'Kechnie's this evening? Just a small party. We have a new medium. An Oriental. A splendid young fellow. You ought to have the experience of hearing him.'

'But I can't just break in like that.'

'Miss M'Kechnie will be very pleased,' said Lipfield. 'Why don't you come? It would be doing us a kindness to increase our numbers.'

'I shan't be able to get there in time. You will want to start at once.'

'On the contrary,' said Lipfield, 'I shall be here for another half-hour. Why not tell Captain Hudson to pick you up at Miss M'Kechnie's? I can run you there in my car.'

'All right.'

'Then I will find you here in about twenty-five minutes' time.'

Lipfield went off, very pleased with himself that he had discovered an additional victim for his séance. I read an evening paper that I found on one of the tables. Hudson came in a minute or two later.

'I was a bit longer than I thought I should be,' he said.

'Lipfield looked in just now. He persuaded me to come to one of his sittings this evening. I shall be let out about the time you want to dine.'

'Where is this happening?'

'At Miss M'Kechnie's. She lives somewhere near Sloane Square. I'll find out the exact address when Lipfield comes to fetch me.'

'And have I got to be there?'

'If I have to wait until ten o'clock for my dinner you must allow me to arrange my own amusements between now and then.'

'I suppose that is just,' Hudson said. 'But I think you are mad. What was it you wanted to tell me?'

'I stayed with the Pimleys the other day to negotiate the sale of the stamps.'

'I said you would.'

'Beryl has found out that Alec is T. T. Waring.'

'How the hell did she do that?'

'Her grandfather died while we were away. She discovered some letters Alec wrote to him. You remember the first T. T. Waring book—about Ceylon?'

'The one he cribbed from a book that had been published in India.'

'Captain Pimley himself wrote it as a young man.'

'But it was anonymous.'

'Probably that was what gave Alec the idea.'

'But if Alec had read his grandfather's book presumably the rest of the family had too.'

'If so, they didn't notice anything.'

'The old man himself must have known.'

'He seems to have thought it a good joke.'

'So the grandfather is dead. Do the rest of the family know about T. T. Waring?'

'Beryl has hidden the letters.'

'What is she going to do about it?'

'Nothing. She just wanted me to tell you. She thought they might help you write the book.'

'Did you tell her the book was off?'

'Yes.'

'Did you give her back the iron?'

'Yes.'

Hudson stood up.

'Good,' he said.

He rolled up the newspaper and tapped it on the table.

'It's not much good doing anything now,' he said.

'What do you mean?'

'Even if one married,' he said, 'wives are only allowed where I'm going for about a month in the year.'

'Perhaps you might graduate to another job.'

'Perhaps,' he said.

'I'm changing my employment too.'

'What? Leaving Judkins & Judkins?'

'I'm going back into advertising.'

We were still discussing our future occupations when Lipfield put his head round the door.

'All ready?' Lipfield said. 'I suppose I can't persuade you to come too, sir? Do you remember what a good evening we had when you last attended?'

'I must stay here,' Hudson said. 'What time will things be over at Miss M'Kechnie's?'

Lipfield made a calculation. He also wrote Miss M'Kechnie's address on the back of one of his visiting-cards. Hudson put the card in his pocket.

'I'll be there,' he said.

As we drove towards the centre of London Lipfield said:

'I promised to take the medium to Miss M'Kechnie's in the car, so we have got to pick him up before going to Sloane Square.'

'Where does the medium live?'

'He has a bed-sitting-room in Bloomsbury. I think you will like him. He is an unassuming young fellow.'

'An Oriental, you said?'

'They sometimes have remarkable powers of clairvoyance,' Lipfield said. 'He was Miss M'Kechnie's discovery. She was staying with friends in the country and he came over to tea. The hostess suggested planchette. Since then he hasn't looked back.'

'Only into the future?'

'Ah, you will have your joke,' said Lipfield. 'You're like Captain Hudson in that way. Well, it's bad news that we are going to lose our adjutant. Field-days won't be the same without him. But I believe he has some private trouble.'

'He has.'

'Sad,' said Lipfield. 'So often happens to the best fellows. Here we are.'

He had stopped the car in front of a house in a long narrow square. There were several bells beside the front door with brass plates or cards stuck above them. Lipfield rang one of the bells. We waited for a time. Lipfield rang again. There was no answer.

'I think one is meant to walk in,' Lipfield said; 'the front door doesn't seem to be locked.'

I followed him into a dark hall that smelt abominably. There was a slab with a lot of dirty letters lying about on it, looking as if they had been there for months, and a staircase straight ahead. A passage led past the staircase to three or four white doors. The noise of several people talking at the top of their voices came from behind one of these. Lipfield said:

'Really I am not sure which one it is. It would never do to walk into the wrong room.'

He stood there for a time, unable to decide what to do next. From the other side of the passage wall the clamour of arguing increased. The voices sounded like those of three women, one of whom was speaking with a strong accent.

'I think this is the one,' Lipfield said.

He knocked. The wrangling died down at once.

'Mr. Lal?' said Lipfield.

The door was opened by a young man. He began explaining something to Lipfield very quickly in a high voice. I did not see that he was an Indian until he turned to the light.

'We must start at once, Mr. Lal,' said Lipfield, 'we are more than a little late already.'

'Very well——'

Mr. Lal paused for a moment as if he could not make up his mind whether or not to invite us into the room. Then he turned away to speak to someone inside. In doing this he took his hand from the door. It swung wide open. A woman was standing behind him, wearing a hat.

'Why, hullo, Beryl!'

Beryl Pimley said nothing. She only stared. Lipfield and Mr. Lal showed relief that Beryl and I should know each other. They both began to talk at the same time. I stepped forward to speak to Beryl and, owing to a flanking movement on the part of Lipfield, found myself within the room. On the other side of the door, a little way to the left and out of sight from the passage, Winefred Pimley was sitting on a chair. She had rather more colour in her face than usual and was watching the scene with her neck craning forward.

'So you are here too, Winefred? I didn't see you.'

'I recognised your voice,' she said.

'I take it,' said Lipfield, 'that these ladies would like to come to the sitting?'

Mr. Lal cast his eyes wildly round on the two sisters. It was apparent that Lipfield and I had interrupted a squabble, presumably caused by Beryl's efforts to persuade Winefred to give up the association. Lal, who was dressed in neatly pressed brown flannel trousers, a blue double-breasted coat, and red-and-white striped tie, looked on the whole a little more robust than most of his countrymen to be seen in that neighbourhood; but the situation presented too difficult a problem for him to offer any immediate solution. He only rolled his eyes and smiled nervously. Winefred got up from her chair.

'I haven't introduced you to my fiancé yet,' she said. 'I suppose you are coming to the sitting too?'

'Winefred——' said Beryl.

Mr. Lal and I shook hands. He showed a lot of white teeth.

'Mr. Lipfield — Miss Winefred Pimley — Miss Beryl Pimley,' he said, 'daughters of Major-General Pimley.'

'Delighted that you two ladies can come,' said Lipfield. 'I don't want to hurry anyone, but really we ought to be going now. Have you got your hat, Mr. Lal?—but, of course, I forgot you never wear one.'

'We are quite ready,' said Winefred.

'I am not going——' began Beryl.

Lipfield looked surprised.

'Tiger is picking me up there at nine-thirty,' I said. 'Why not come and have a word with him after? I know he'd like to see you.'

'Is Tiger going to be there?' said Winefred.

'He is only arriving at the end. We are dining together.'

'Then you must certainly come,' Winefred said.

She took her sister by the arm. Beryl shook her off. Winefred was insistent.

'You must come,' she said. 'Why are you being so silly? You know you want to see Tiger again.'

'He certainly wants to see you,' I said. 'It's the last chance there will be, because he leaves the country early next week.'

'Does he?'

'Come along, please,' said Lipfield.

He went off down the passage, followed by Mr. Lal and Winefred. Beryl was still hesitating. She made a move as if to go with them. We were left alone together in the room.

'What's been happening here?'

'I came up to London for the night to see my dentist. I was trying to prevent her from meeting Lal again when you arrived,' she said.

222

'You'd better come with us now.'

'All right. I will.'

We all crammed into Lipfield's car. Beryl sat in front and the rest of us at the back with Winefred in the middle between Lal and myself. Lal leaned across.

'You often come to sittings?'

'Only once before.'

'He-he-he,' he said.

Winefred sat in silence most of the way. Towards the end of the journey she said:

'How did you turn out to be with Lipfield?'

'I met him down at the Territorial headquarters and came along with him.'

'I'm glad you did.'

'There seemed to be a clash of temperaments in progress.

'Beryl was trying to interfere.'

'But where does Lipfield come in? I thought your fiancé was at the R.M.C.?'

'He left there. He decided that he would do better out of the Army with his exceptional psychic gifts.'

'Useful qualities in the Directorate of Military Intelligence.'

Winefred did not answer. She moved a little further away on the seat. Neither of us spoke again until we arrived at our destination.

The nature of the entertainment offered at Miss M'Kechnie's was of a less professional order than the same thing at Mrs. Cromwell's. The room was small. There was a lot of flowered cretonne everywhere and some silhouettes in black-and-gold frames. A circle of chairs had been arranged in the drawing-room, where Miss M'Kechnie herself was waiting with an elderly white-haired woman whom I recognised as having been present at Mrs. Cromwell's séance. Miss M'Kechnie seemed on the whole pleased that the gathering had increased in number from unexpected sources.

'I sent a card to Mr. Judkins,' she said, 'but I haven't seen him for some time. I think he must be away.'

'He won't come,' said Lipfield. 'I can tell you that, Miss M'Kechnie.'

'Why not?'

'Because he doesn't approve any longer.'

'He hasn't approved,' said Miss M'Kechnie, 'for years. However, he is usually punctual, so perhaps he has another engagement.'

'I think he may be in Scotland,' I said. 'He was going there when I last heard of him.'

'In that case,' said Miss M'Kechnie, 'we need not wait. How are you feeling, Mr. Lal? Do you think you will be in the vein?'

In these friendly surroundings Lal seemed to be recovering his composure. I did not know for how long a time before Lipfield and I had arrived he had had to undergo Beryl's lecturings. It must have been long enough to work him up into a state of considerable nervous discomfort.

'I will do my best,' he said. 'I am not feeling so well as I do sometimes. Perhaps we might try singing Kipling's *Recessional* first.'

'With the piano?' said Miss M'Kechnie. 'Shall I play, Mr. Lal?'

'No. I would rather you did not play.'

'Or what about *Keep the Home Fires Burning?*' said the woman with the white hair. 'You were wonderful, Mr. Lal, the night we sang that.'

'Very well, then. *Keep the Home Fires Burning.*' Lal smiled gently.

'If you begin to feel the slightest strain,' Winefred said, 'you must stop. After all, you have been through a great deal this evening.'

She glared across the room at Beryl. Winefred's manner when she spoke to Lal was not much different from her way of addressing anyone else. If anything, her gruffness was stressed to imply ownership.

The arranging of the room took some time to complete. Just before the light was extinguished the front-door bell rang.

'I wonder who that is?' Miss M'Kechnie said.

Everyone who knew him was surprised when Hugh Judkins was shown into the room.

'You are rather late, Mr. Judkins,' said Miss M'Kechnie, 'so we were going to begin without you.'

Hugh took hardly any notice of her. He was not looking himself yet. His suit hung on him as if he had been using it for some weeks as pyjamas, and his tie was riding up at the back of his collar. He allowed himself to be introduced to Lal and the Pimleys. Lipfield said 'Good-evening, Mr. Judkins' in a marked mannner, but Hugh seemed not to hear him. An extra chair was needed, and one with a cork seat had to be brought in from the bathroom.

'How are you feeling, Hugh?' I said, when this had been done.

'Well,' he said. 'Why?'

The faint hairs that shimmered on the top of his head in an irregular mossy covering gave him, with the light behind him, more than ever the appearance of having a halo. One expected him to be carrying a gridiron or some other instruments of martyrdom like a saint in a stained-glass window.

Miss M'Kechnie put out all the lights except one small

globe with a red covering of rubber. Lal sat between Miss M'Kechnie and Winefred; then Hugh, the white-haired woman, myself, Beryl, and Lipfield, who completed the circle by holding Winefred's other hand. Beryl, like Hugh, moved as one in a dream. In the car Lipfield's battery of small talk seemed to have made her forget the scene at Lal's lodgings. Now she appeared to have no idea why we were all at Miss M'Kechnie's nor what we proposed to do there. Soon after arrival she had said:

'And is Tiger really coming?'

'Yes,' I told her, 'when this is over.'

When she felt certain of this she settled down as if she were prepared to go through with anything that might be required of her.

Proceedings opened slowly. Lal went off into a comatose state. We sang a little and waited. Nothing happened. We sang again. Beryl joined in the singing quite loudly. She may have thought that it was an end in itself. A long silence followed our last burst of singing.

This was broken at length by Lal himself. He heaved about for a time on his chair. Then he rubbed his eyes and stretched as if he had just got out of bed.

'I am afraid I have not the right disposition tonight,' he said. 'Something has upset me.'

'Poor Mr. Lal,' said Miss M'Kechnie. 'Is there anything we can do?'

'Thank you, no. I will tell you what. Tonight I will just be clairvoyant.'

'Oh, but that will be so tiring for you, Mr. Lal,' said the woman with the white hair.

'Never mind,' said Lal, 'never mind. I do not like to bring disappointment to a house.'

And so we let go of each other's hands and waited again. Lal returned to his chair. He relaxed. While he was relaxing he passed his fingers lightly over his forehead as if feeling for invisible spots on the surface of the skin. He continued to do this for some minutes. Then he began to speak:

'. . . There is amongst us here tonight one who sits surrounded by many volumes . . . he has a great library . . . this man . . . he is about forty or fifty years old . . . brings with him an uneasy spirit . . .'

Lal waited so long after saying this before he spoke again that I thought he had fallen asleep. Then at last his voice came from the shades.

'. . . I see this spirit . . . it takes the shape of a man who wears the habit of the East. . . . He is by the side of the water and he writes in a book . . .'

Lal paused.

'. . . The scene is changing . . . as it were smoke drifts past . . . the figures are lost . . .'

In the gloom Hugh could be seen putting his right hand in front of his mouth, supporting the elbow with his left palm.

'. . . The clouds clear . . .' Lal's voice was firm. . . . 'I see the first man in his library . . . he reads . . . and reads . . . and reads . . . his servants bring a book to him . . . and another . . . and another . . . and another . . . and another . . . they are the books in which the man has written who sits by the waters of the seashore clad in the garb of the East . . . the picture grows dim . . .'

There was a period of several minutes before Lal found an opportunity to assemble the component parts of the new vision.

'. . . I see an old, old man . . . he scans a letter . . . it is from the man who writes in the books by the blue water . . . the old man goes to his treasure . . . he takes a bag . . . the bag is full of gold . . .'

There was silence. The woman with the white hair blew her nose. Miss M'Kechnie sighed. Lal said:

'. . . The old man sends gold . . . yes . . . to the man by the sea . . . they are kin, the one with another . . . the man in his library spreads the word of the man by the sea . . . he goes into the highways and byways . . . holding above his head the books of the man in the garb of the East. . . . The people——'

Suddenly there was a tremendous disturbance. In the dark it was not possible to see how it arose. Hugh's voice shouted:

'I protest.'

Almost the same moment I realised that Beryl had left her seat and was standing over Winefred, shaking her, and saying:

'*You* must have told him—*you* must have told him.'

'Turn the light on,' said Miss M'Kechnie.

Somebody did this. There was general disintegration. Everyone stood up. Hugh said again:

'I *protest*, Miss M'Kechnie.'

Whoever had started the trouble—I suspected it was Beryl—Miss M'Kechnie had determined to fix the blame on Hugh.

'*You* protest, Mr. Judkins?' she said. 'When Mr. Lal was in the middle of one of the most remarkable pieces of clairvoyance I have ever listened to. I am surprised that you do not know better. Surely you must realise how dangerous it is for a subject to be disturbed in this way? How do you feel, Mr. Lal?'

She turned in Lal's direction. Before Lal could answer, Hugh stepped across the room and took Miss M'Kechnie's arm.

'I make no apology,' he said, 'for putting an end to this parade of superstition.'

'Mr. Judkins,' said Miss M'Kechnie, 'you have gone too far.'

She had not seen Hugh in the office, and obviously she had no idea of the change that had taken place in him since the earlier part of the summer. To her this behaviour was no more than an extension of Hugh's habitual aggressiveness on the subject of occult matters.

'If you talk like this,' she said, 'you will have to leave my house.'

She spoke as if she was glad to have an opportunity to pronounce authoritatively on this matter. Lipfield had come up behind her in support. Beryl and Winefred were still having a violent argument in the corner. No one took any notice of them; but, so far as I could hear, Winefred was hotly denying ever having mentioned T. T. Waring to Lal in any capacity whatsoever.

'I should never have invited you,' Miss M'Kechnie said, 'if I had expected this. Though I must say you have often given me cause to complain in the past.'

Hugh stood in front of her holding the lapels of his coat and listening. His mouth worked all the time. Suddenly he began to speak, so quickly and fiercely that it was hard to catch what he was saying.

'I came here tonight, Miss M'Kechnie, to ask you—to beg you—to turn away from these abominations. That was the sole reason for my presence. I wanted to choose my moment. I had intended to wait until all was over and then reason with you on the futility' and wickedness of such an evening as this. But then a subject was referred to—you cannot pretend that such a reference was not intended—to a figure that once meant much to me. I speak of course of T. T. Waring. How this Indian knew of him and his connection with me I do not attempt to explain. All I know is that he should not have possessed such knowledge. Drive such men away from your doors. Why must you commune with evil spirits? Remember Mrs. Cromwell. Forsake the road that leads to hell and Bedlam.'

Hugh made a movement with his elbow in the direction of Lal.

'How dare you, Mr. Judkins!' Miss M'Kechnie said.

'Now listen, Judkins——' said Lipfield.

Suddenly Lal jumped to his feet. He placed his hands on Hugh's shoulders.

'My dear sir,' he said, 'you employ a positively mediaeval phraseology. Why should you suppose that psychical research should have these deleterious effects?'

Hugh seemed taken aback. He always showed a horror of being touched by anyone. Shirley Handsworth had once put his arm round Hugh's shoulders when he had been standing beside Hugh's chair reading a clause in a contract; Hugh had writhed nearly out of his seat. Now he wriggled away from Lal as if the Indian's hands were red-hot.

'I know what you are going to reply,' said Lal. 'You are going to say that we are dealing with matters that have always been regarded as being culpable—even diabolical— matters ignored by the general-staff of the march of science.'

'I object——' said Hugh.

'You object, my dear sir, because you are full of prejudice on the subject.'

Lal had a quick, clipped way of talking that would have irritated Hugh at his most self-controlled. In Hugh's present state anything might happen if Lal continued to speak to him in this manner. Even now he was not far from fury. Unless something was done quickly he might even attack Lal with his hands. He was catching his breath and shaking from side to side. An exterior force put a sudden end to this situation. The door of the drawing-room opened and the maid said:

'Captain Hudson.'

Miss M'Kechnie was standing a short way in front of the door as Hudson came in, so that when she turned she was the first person present he saw. He said at once:

'I hope I haven't arrived too early. Your maid said that as the lights were on in the drawing-room it would be all right if she showed me in.'

'Quite all right,' said Miss M'Kechnie. 'We are all very glad to see you.'

Hudson looked round the room. He saw Lipfield and Hugh and Winefred and Beryl. He gave each of them the same embarrassed nod.

'Let me see, Captain Hudson,' said Miss M'Kechnie, 'I don't know how many of these people you have met. Not Mr. Lal, I think.'

She had kept her head well. So had Winefred. Lal held out his hand.

'No, not now,' Winefred said. 'You will have plenty of time to meet later. We must go. Thank you very much, Miss M'Kechnie. It has been a delightful evening.'

She and Lal were gone before any more could be said. Hudson went slowly across to Beryl and they began to talk together. Lipfield said to Hugh:

'Look here, Judkins, don't you think you ought to be getting off to bed? You're not looking at all well.'

Hugh laughed. He passed his hand over the back of his head and took off his pince-nez and began to polish them.

'I'm afraid I was making rather a fool of myself,' he said. 'I shouldn't allow myself to get so excited. My doctor specially warned me against it. It is absurd to pay a physician if you don't take his advice. Though I must say one often knows what is wrong far sooner than they do.'

He spoke just as he used to.

'I think I will be getting back,' he said.

The white-haired woman, who seemed less affected than anyone by the scene that had taken place, was talking earnestly with Miss M'Kechnie in the corner of the room. Hugh said:

'I think I will slip away now and write Miss M'Kechnie a note in the morning. Can I give anyone a lift?'

'I've got my own car here, thanks, Judkins,' Lipfield said.

As Hugh went through the door Hudson came up and said:

'I say, do you mind if we don't have dinner together to-night? I think I am going to take Beryl somewhere.'

'All right.'

'Sure you don't mind?'

'Quite sure.'

'Well, good-bye,' said Hudson. 'I'll write and tell you what it is like out there.'

'Do.'

He shook hands and returned to Beryl.

'Would you care to sample a sandwich with me at the Automobile Club?' Lipfield said.

'I'd like to very much.'

We said good-night to Miss M'Kechnie. She and the white-haired woman had decided that a cup of tea would be nice. Lipfield and I refused this with thanks. Later, in the club, Lipfield told me about some of the awkward episodes he had experienced when organising sittings. There were a great many of them, and their description occupied the rest of the evening until it was time for bed.

10

It must have been towards Christmas in the same year. I had been working on *Stendhal: and Some Thoughts on Violence* after dinner and had gone to bed at about half-past eleven. I was just dropping off to sleep when the telephone-bell rang.

'Hullo?'

'She's dead,' said a man's voice.

'Who is?'

'Great-aunt Theodora.'

'I think you have the wrong number.'

'Aren't you interested in death?'

'Not specially.'

'I am.'

'Who are you?'

'Captain Bromwich speaking, sir.'

'Eustace.'

'I-thank-you-for-leave-to-speak-sir, but an elderly relative of mine has passed away. I've come over to collect the dough.'

'When did you arrive?'

'This afternoon.'

'Where are you staying?'

'At my fiancée's flat.'

'Your fiancée?'

'You didn't know I was engaged, did you?'

'I don't believe it.'

'She is a friend of yours.'

233

'She has let me down this time.'

'Guess who.'

'I won't. It would compromise an innocent girl if I guessed wrong.

'Miss Roberta Payne.'

'Congratulations.'

'You don't seem to think it funny.'

'I'm in bed and half-asleep.'

'Very well, you're excused. How have you been?'

'I've got a new job. I'm back in advertising.'

'I see that Judkins & Judkins published the posthumous T. T. Waring.'

'They didn't have the benefit of his showmanship this time. The sales were down. The notices weren't so good either.'

'That won't bother him where he is.'

'I don't expect literary reviews abound in the Greek islands.'

'Why the Greek islands?'

'That was where T. T. Waring was going when we last met him.'

'You mean to say I never told you?'

'What?'

'The *Amphitrite* ran aground the night of that storm. Somewhere on the coast above St. Etienne. They only managed to save the nigger. He's working now at a bar in Toulon. I often go there.'

'And Alec Pimley and Mrs. Cromwell were drowned?'

'Poor old girl,' said Eustace. 'With all her faults I regret her profoundly. You know, I believe she was the widow of the beggar who cut off Charles the First's head. She seemed to me to have something on her conscience. She was always wanting to atone.'

'I suppose it is a certainty this time.'

'Sad that their married life should have ended in that way. It might have lasted for several years.'

'I must write and tell Tiger.'

'What happened to that bright boy?'

'He joined the Camel Corps.'

'Did he patch it up with his girl?'

'They got married. She's in Kenya at the moment.'

'Fine. Roberta tells me she upset your late boss a lot up among the fjords.'

'So much so that he decided to become a schoolmaster again.'

'I'll tell her that. When are we going to see you?'

'Shall I come round tomorrow?'

'About six-thirty. I'll show you the cutting about the wreck of the *Amphitrite*. What's that? Roberta says come earlier—about six.'

Eustace rang off. I turned over in the bed. Now would be a good time to sleep. The preliminary efforts were unsuccessful. Some people were leaving the house opposite, making a lot of noise saying good-night. Then everything was quiet. It would be easy to drop off in a minute or two now. In the square round the corner the church clock struck the hour; and the next; and the next. Thoughts about Stendhal. What sort of a time had he had when one came to examine it? *The Life and Sentiments of Silencious Harry.* Were his political ambitions a form of romanticism? Napoleon worship. Those women. Why had he felt so strongly about trimming plane trees? His schooldays. The masters had been a funny crowd. French. How was Hugh getting on at his old profession? It was power Hugh wanted too. Everybody wanted power. Bernard wanted power. Lipfield wanted power. Roberta wanted power. T. T. Waring wanted power. Did Eustace want power? It was an interesting question. Was money power? And then there was that letter about income tax waiting for an answer. Would it help to count sheep or to turn hymns into French? One kept on getting back to France. Life had been pleasant at Toulon. But Mrs. Cromwell had wanted power. Winefred wanted power too. Lal wanted power. That was why he left Sandhurst. T. T. Waring. He wanted power more than any of them. Curious how that poem must have struck him. *In Vishnuland what Avatar?* The Pimleys might have said that to Lal. It was no good trying to sleep. Soon the morning would get light. Power. The milk arrived in the street, making a great clatter. T. T. Waring . . . Sleep, like a long drink, came at last.